WAIT FOR ME

WRITTEN BY

J. J. VALENTIN

This is a work of fiction. All the characters and events
portrayed in this novel are fictitious.

WAIT FOR ME

Dedicated to my mom

WAIT FOR ME

CHAPTER ONE

∞

My sweet Sadie, today makes seventy three. I'm an old man now, but I still thrive with a young, foolish heart for you. Every day I sit here and think about you, and every day I die a little more from the thought of knowing you're not here. But as the dusk fades out and the dawn rolls in, I can still feel you in the soft blows of the wind, gentle as ever. Oh, what I would do to see you agai—

"Excuse me. Excuse me, sir."

"Huh?"

"I'm sorry, didn't mean to startle you. I didn't realize you were asleep."

"Oh, no, it's quite all right. I wasn't sleeping. I just got lost in the moment, I suppose. I like to close my eyes and take in the cool breeze that blows in and out of those meadows every morning. It refreshes my soul. I must've dozed off for a minute. What can I do for you? Are you lost?"

"Not any more than you."

"Well, I don't normally get visitors—especially not at this hour. What can I do for you?"

"I'm new in town and some nice folk at the market told me that you like to sit out here every morning to watch the sunrise. I, myself, enjoy waking before the dawn and soaking in the refreshing life that rises with it. I'm also a photographer, so not only do I enjoy the peace of the morning, like you, I can also appreciate the beauty in the sound of the chirping birds and the colors that collide in the sky—it's all living art to me. There's nothing quite like it."

"Indeed, there isn't. It's my favorite time of day. I haven't missed a sunrise since ... well, let's just say it's been a while."

"I see. By the way my name is Sa—"

"Sami is it? It's nice to meet you, darling. I'm Mr. Harrison, but you can call me—"

"Nicholi."

"Yes ... Nicholi. How did you know?"

"Folks at the market told me."

"I sure must be famous over there. There seems to be a lot of chatter about me."

"I was looking for a friend and they said you might be,

too."

"No offense, darling, but you and I could not be friends. I'm an old man and you but started your life. Plus, I could see the truth behind your lie. I assume you really came to snap some shots. There's no need to try and butter me up. Be my guest. You can stay here as long as you need."

"Thank you, Nicholi."

"You're very welcome. I must admit it's nice to have some company for once. I haven't seen a fresh face in, well, God knows when. Time around here seems to past by me. Here, take a seat. It's a bit dusty on this porch. I hope you don't mind. It's how I like it—organic, in a way. It's rundown and creaks with every step, just like its owner."

"I don't mind at all. I like it this way, as well."

"Well, feel free to start snapping away. I have to run in for a minute. That tea's been whistling for me for quite some time. I've been battling this cold for a while. It doesn't want to release its grip on me. Sometimes, I feel like it's won. But, surprisingly, right now I feel better than I had in a while. It's got to be this tea—or perhaps it's your company. I bet it's the latter. Would you like a cup, darling?"

"Don't make me blush, Nicholi. Sure, I'd love a cup."

"Honey or lemon?"

"Honey."

"Ah, just how I like it, especially on a cool morning like

today. 'The honey soothes the demons that try to strep your throat,' my mother used to say. I'll be right back."

Oh, Sadie, you've sent me company. I know it's your work. My eyes have aged and become nearly blind, yet I can tell that she resembles you in every way. From her long black hair to that smile that brightens the darkest of nights and somehow manages to pass through my glaucoma—even her voice has me clutching at my heart. Don't worry, darling, you're never forgotten. I've come back home to be with you.

"Here you go. I hope you enjoy it. I grew the leaves myself."

"Thank you, Nicholi. I'm sure it'll be the best cup I'll ever have."

"Oh, sweet lies you tell. It's satisfactory at best. I've only been growing the Camellia sinensis a few months now. I'm trying something new to keep this old man occupied and his motors running, you know? Plus, there's only so much time I can spend reminiscing on this porch before my ass gets upset with me. Don't be shy to spit it up if you don't like it. It's hard to come across critique nowadays, so please tell me what you think."

"Lies, I assure you, I do not tell, Nicholi. I'm certain this will be the best cup I'll ever have, and you know why? Because it's with you, a *good*, *kind* man—who may, one day, come to the marketplace with me."

"You know, you're the first to ever try it."

"First? How so?"

"In case you haven't looked around, there aren't many people living in these woods. It's just me and the wilderness."

"No family?"

"It's complicated."

"Where is your wife?"

"We've come to a mutual understanding that it was time I came back home, alone."

"I see. What about that house over there? You don't speak to your neighbors?"

"Where?"

"Right over there, just past the tall grass. It can't be more than 100 yards from here. I'm sure they'd love a cup. Why don't you invite them over for some?"

"No. I can't. I'm fine right over here."

"Can't? If there is one thing I know, it's that *can't* is nothing more than denial. If you're too afraid to approach them, I'd gladly break the ice and go over for you. Who knows, you might be able to make a friend or two."

"No, please don't. Like I said, I'm just fine right over here."

"Come on, Nicholi, you can do it. *Don't be shy*. Everyone needs a friend."

"*I said no!* Now please ... just leave it alone, okay?"

"I'm sorry. I didn't mean to upset you. I only thought you might be lonely, that's all."

"I just can't go over there. I hope you can understand that."

"I understand. Everyone has their issues. If you'd like to talk about yours, I'm all ears."

"You're right. Everyone does have their *own* issues, so there's no need to burden you with mine. It's a long story, anyway, a story that won't do you any good. There's no need to hear this old man babble about his life."

"I haven't had anyone to talk to in a while, to be honest. It would be refreshing and a pleasure to learn more about you. *I'm a good listener.*"

She's more like you than I could have imagined. Although her image and voice brings you back to life, it is her persistence that has you both matched. You're not forgotten, Sadie.

"Nicholi, are you listening to me?"

"Huh? Oh, yes. Sorry, I got lost in my own thoughts. Do you really want to know my story? Are you sure?"

"I do. You know they say it's good to talk about your problems. It gets rid of the pain in the heart and allows that space to be filled with something more fruitful."

"That home ..."

"Talk to me."

"That home, just past the tall grass, has destroyed my life, yet given me one. It has tortured me, yet I'm indebted to it. It *consumes* me with pain, yet I'd give up my entire life just to have another minute with the girl who once lived in it."

CHAPTER TWO

∞

Every day started just as today, with me sitting on this porch—except both it and I were young and fresh back then. I was a 12-year-old boy, and it was a sanded-down, freshly painted white oak. During the early mornings, as I sat on this porch, I looked up at the starry sky and allowed my mind to wander. Some days, I dreamed as any other young boy would—I'd fantasize that I was a superhero on a quest to save the world. But most days, I simply wanted to save her.

I'd daydream to pass the time until the light in the second story of that house turned on, because I knew just a few minutes later—like clockwork—the tall grass would sway and then she'd come forth. It was our routine every morning. We never missed a sunrise together before the school day started, no matter what. And as we waited for the sun to come up, I'd tell her stories—stories that filled her with bliss. She loved them. It was a means for her to escape reality, even if it was only for a moment. My stories gave her hope, and for me, they gave me a chance to see her smile. Every time I'd tell her a new story, I'd wait anxiously for that smile that was missing, that smile that remained dormant, that smile that I remembered seeing before Mr. Coughlin came back ... that smile that had become a distant memory.

I loved Sadie before I even knew the definition of love. She was my best friend. We grew up together and thought we'd grow old together, even our mothers were best of friends. Mrs. Coughlin, Sadie's mother, would bring her over to my house every day since infancy. We were stitched together from the start. We could've had a perfect life ... but hell decided to lay its foundation in her home when the devil himself came back to rest.

Mr. Coughlin, Mrs. Coughlin's husband, had been a soldier in the Great War. During his earlier terms, he'd come home every now and then (not for long), and when he did, Sadie was elated. He was her hero. He was her favorite person in the world—and she was his. He was a good man once, but something changed as she got older.

PTSD, Mrs. Coughlin said was to blame for the anger that consumed her husband when he returned home after being medically discharged. His abuse started just as many do—verbally. He'd start petty arguments with Mrs. Coughlin and then redirect them at Sadie as if she was the cause. Most arguments began at dinnertime since he'd spend most of his day either at work or at the bar. Sadie said she'd have to wait until he finished his dinner in order to eat, and by that time, her food was already cold. Her mother would offer to heat it up, but then Mr. Coughlin would fuss about the gas bill and how they couldn't afford to reheat food because "the child is too stubborn to eat it warm." The man that once held my sweet Sadie tightly in his arms and swore to protect her against anything and everything became a man that despised her, and the hero Sadie once beloved more than anything became her monster. While it is common for children to fear boogeymen through their own imagination, Sadie's boogeyman was in the flesh. She didn't have the privilege to fear imaginary monsters because hers rested within her home. She feared Mr. Coughlin so much that she was even too afraid to go to the bathroom in the middle of the night because then she'd have to flush the toilet and didn't want to wake him, so she'd pee in a plastic bowl and wait until the morning to dump it. My sweet Sadie was a prisoner in her own home. And to make things worse, the misery she felt at home spilled over into school, because she never had sufficient school supplies and was one of the few who were forced to eat from the cafeteria instead of having a homemade meal, like my mother made for me and most children's parents made for them.

I knew I couldn't stop the pain she felt at home, but I'd be damned to sit back and witness her misery at school, so I gave Sadie half of whatever my mother prepared for me for lunch every day—sometimes I gave it all to her, depending on how hungry she was—and I told my parents that I needed twice the amount of school supplies than I did. They weren't ignorant to what I was doing, but they didn't say anything, either. They provided what I needed, but that's as far as they went. They never got their hands dirty.

I did what I could to help my Sadie, but there was nothing I could do for her after what I would accidently learn one day at school. During lunch, I noticed something I hadn't before. It suddenly dawned on me. It was 95 degrees outside, yet Sadie was wearing a long shirt and pants. I realized then that she *always* wore long shirts and pants, so I asked her about it, and she said she was anemic—something her mother must have coached her to say—so she was always cold. That didn't sit right with me. I knew she was lying. She told me everything, except for this. She felt ashamed and weak, as many victims do.

On that same day, two periods after lunch, she was walking down the hall with her books in her hands when a girl thought it'd be funny to slap them to the ground. Sadie was constantly bullied at school because, in their words, she was "weird." I was across the hall at my locker at the time when

I saw a crowd gather and heard my peers chuckling. When I realized it was Sadie that they were laughing at, I ran over and defended her. I used every word in the forsaken language, but then ... I became speechless. As Sadie was picking up her books, her shirt rose up a little on her back and revealed a long horizontal belt mark, and I could see another just peaking beneath the bottom of her shirt at her side. No one else but I saw it, because no one bothered to truly look at her. They viewed her like a dog, but she hypnotized me daily. When I looked at her, no matter how long or quick, whether it was a stare or glance, I always took in everything because she meant *everything* to me. But on that day, I took in more than I wanted. I took in a sight that would haunt me even to this day.

I didn't say anything to her about it because she was already on the verge of tears, and quite frankly, I didn't know what to say. I just helped her pick up her books and continued to scold everyone who laughed around us.

I went home in tears that day, and I tried to get help from my parents, but they were a timid, don't-see-nothing, won't-say-nothing type of people. And even when evidence was brought to their doorstep—like Sadie—they turned a blind eye to it. It was either "their family's dispute," or "no one can tell a man how to raise his own child." My parents were cowards. They never fought the good fight, just swayed like the tall grass.

Three days later, early Monday morning, I as always, sat on this porch, stared at my watch and waited for the tall grass to sway. As I waited, I couldn't help but remember those marks on Sadie's back, and I became anxious with every minute that passed because she was late. My gut told me something was wrong. It wasn't like her to be late.

Eventually, the tall grass did sway and out she came … limping. She had a busted lip, and the clothes that normally hid her bruises were now torn, revealing even more.

I stood up in horror, and she put her head between my neck and shoulder and let out all of the years of her agony in a single gasp for air. Her body shivered, and she cried with an immense struggle to breathe. To this day, I've never seen someone cry the way she did. No story that I could've ever told her would have taken away that pain, so I did the only thing I thought would help: I grabbed her by the hand to bring her inside my house to see my parents. But she held back.

"*Come on*, Sadie," I said, not accepting no for an answer.

She shook her head, refusing to come in.

"My parents will help you. *They have to.*"

She looked back at her home and then at me. She did this several times until she finally agreed.

"Mom! Dad!" I yelled out for them, entering my home. They were having coffee in the kitchen when I walked in with Sadie. My mother's cup fell over and coffee spilled over the counter.

"What happened to you?" my mother asked.

"Mr. Coughlin hurt her."

Rather than immediately come to Sadie's aide, she had the audacity to ask a question that *still* angers me. "What did you do?"

I could see in Sadie's eyes that she was actually thinking about what she may have done wrong. "*Stop it*, Sadie," I said, nudging her. "You didn't do anything."

I then looked at my mother with disgust. "*She didn't do anything!*"

"I'll speak with your mom today," my mother told her.

"What good would that do? You told me you always talk to her," I said.

My mother looked away.

"You haven't, have you?"

"It's a complicated situation, Nicky."

My mother turned to Sadie and stretched out her hand. "Come here, sweetie. Let me clean you up."

"To send her back?" I antagonized.

Sadie looked at my mother and finally spoke. "I'll b-be fine. I should g-go back home now." Her voice kept breaking, and my heart along with it. "My dad already left, s-so I'll be fine. I'm going to g-go to bed. My mom said I could stay home today. I-I just didn't want to keep Nicky waiting, t-that's all."

My mother sighed.

I looked to my father for help, but he remained seated and shook his head.

"Dad, you have to do *something*."

"There's nothing we can do, Nicky. Mr. and Mrs. Coughlin are good friends of ours. All we can do is talk to them."

"What is there to talk about!" I shouted. I didn't understand why they were choosing to look away from what was so clearly in front of them.

With her head down, Sadie walked out the door, and I chased after her.

"Sadie, wait!"

She turned around right before entering the tall grass. Her eyes stared blankly at me. There was no one to turn to, no one to help. She was a tortured prisoner on her way back to her warden.

"I'm going to help you," I said. "I'm going to call the police."

Her eyes nearly jumped out of her face. "Don't! Please don't do that, Nicky."

"Why? They will help you."

"They'll take me away."

"Good. Let them take you away."

She shook her head, and her chest caved in as if what I had said broke her heart. "No, Nicky. Promise me you won't do that."

"Why, Sadie? Why don't you let me help you?"

"They'll take me away, Nicky. They'll take me away ... *from you*. You're the only friend I have."

There was nothing I could say or do. She was right. I was forced to watch Sadie willingly walk back into hell. We were two different children, in two different homes, yet both broken. I stormed up the stairs and slammed my door shut. If I were to do that on any other day, my parents would have punished me for a week. But I heard no complaint. Silence was welcomed in my home that day.

I didn't get to tell her a story, I thought, as I lied in bed trying to think of ways to save her. I needed to make her feel better, and this was the only way I knew how.

In that moment, an idea came to mind. I jumped up from my bed, went into my closet and pulled out my walkie-talkies and then I went back downstairs, out the side door, and through the tall grass. When I arrived at her house, I picked up pebbles and gently through them up at her window.

Sadie, confused, quietly opened her window.

"Take this," I mouthed, lifting one walkie-talkie into the air.

"How?" she mouthed back.

I had one shot to throw the walkie-talkie through her window, and she had one shot to catch it or else we risked breaking it. Luckily, my aim was dead on and her hands were flawless. I jumped up and celebrated like a quarter-back who had just thrown the winning touchdown, and Sadie shook her head in delight.

With a hand signal, I told her that I'd call her later. She nodded, and I went back through the tall grass, into my house, and into my room. I sat by the window and dialed her in almost immediately.

Sadie was a huge fan of black-and-white films. She loved how the men were gentlemen and how elegantly the women dressed. She especially loved when the men called their women darling.

"Hello, darling," I said. "Do you want to hear a story?"

She giggled. "Yes, please."

I improvised for over an hour while she lied in bed comfortably and listened, and when she didn't respond after a while, I knew she had fallen peacefully asleep. I had done my job. I had been the one thing she knew she could count on; I had been her friend.

Her rest gave me rest, and since I knew she was dreaming, I wanted to join her, so I slept.

When I woke up in the afternoon, I spent the day daydreaming about saving Sadie. I fantasized about being as big in stature as Mr. Coughlin and matching his strength, ultimately rescuing my darling and flying away with her in my arms. I rode my bicycle to simulate the flying, and I rode through areas I never dared to enter before.

I rode and rode and rode until I hit a dead end, sort of. This "dead end" was actually a freight train passing by.

I wondered where it was going. I wished Sadie and I were on it. I wished we could ride it into the sunset rather than watch the sunrise in the morning. I was tired of the cycle of misery, so I let out a scream from the core of my belly that, from my ears, matched the train's steel grinding on the rails. I let it all out, so much that I shook.

I watched trains pass for many hours. I could've watched them for days if only the sun had frozen in place, but when I saw that it was beginning to set, I was forced to head back home.

When I got home, dinner was ready for me on the table, and my parents had welcoming expressions on their faces as if nothing had happened. They always swept their problems under the rug. I couldn't bear to eat dinner with them, so I went directly to my room. I couldn't understand how two loving parents could not show the same affection they had for me to another child in need. I didn't understand how their friendships were more important than the safety of Sadie.

When I entered my room, I looked out of my window at Sadie's home. I saw her light on, and I wondered what she was doing, so I dialed her in.

"Sadie?"

No answer.

"Sadie. Over."

No answer.

It was likely that she was just not around when I was calling, but I was worried sick.

5 minutes went by, 15 minutes went by, 30 minutes ... an hour. I dialed her in again. *"Sadie. Over."*

All I heard on my end was static.

She's fine. Mr. Coughlin isn't home yet, I told myself.

Around 11 that night, my walkie-talkie beeped.

"Nicky, are you up? Over."

I jumped out of bed and picked up. "Sadie! Where've you been?"

For the first time in a long time, I heard bliss in her voice. She actually had a good day. Since Mr. Coughlin had been gone, Sadie's mother made the day all about her. She felt terrible about what her husband had done to Sadie and tried her best to make it up to her. They ate breakfast together, watched movies, sang and danced, and Sadie was now resting in clean sheets and fresh blankets. Her world had done a complete 180.

I told her about my day—leaving out the anger and worry I felt—and how I watched huge freight trains zoom past me. I also told her that I almost got lost on the way back, and she laughed at me. Oh that laugh ... I hadn't heard it in a long time.

"See you tomorrow? Same time?" I asked.

"Same time as always, Nich—" she paused mid-sentence after noticing Mr. Coughlin's car pull up to the driveway. The only reason for him being gone all day would have been because he went to the bar after work. And he became a monster when he drank. "I have to go, Nicky. I'll see you tomorrow."

I grabbed my binoculars from my closet and focused them on Sadie's home.

Mr. Coughlin walked into the house, and the light on the first floor turned on. Mrs. Coughlin appeared in the center of the three windows speaking to him. She was moving her hands in a way of suggesting that he should calm down. I thought it had worked because I saw him grab her and passionately kiss her, but then he threw her to the side. He then moved out of sight, but I tracked him through the windows. I followed his every move until the lights shut off. Unable to see him anymore, I turned my attention to Sadie's room. She had turned off her light as soon as she saw him arrive; she was pretending to be asleep.

Turn on, I said, wishing to see Mr. and Mrs. Coughlin's room light up because then I'd know Mr. Coughlin was going to bed and Sadie would be fine.

But I didn't get that wish. It was Sadie's room that lit up, and I knew what that meant. Mr. Coughlin entered her room, and she jumped out of bed. She held the walkie-talkie behind her back as she stepped as far away from him as she could. Eventually, she ran out of room and backed herself into the windowsill. She was like prey backed into a corner waiting for the lion to strike; she was defenseless. Her walkie-talkie must have accidentally leaned against the windowsill because she dialed me in. I heard everything—every word, every breath.

"Papa, please don't hurt me," she said. "I'm sorry."

There was nothing for her to be sorry about, but she was used to apologizing.

Mr. Coughlin threw a fit. I couldn't make out his words. Everything he said was slurred.

My body began to shake. *Don't touch her,* I said beneath my breath. *Don't touch her.*

Mr. Coughlin began loosening his belt, and Sadie turned to her side.

My eyes narrowed in on him, as if staring at him so intensely would stop him. But it didn't. He hit her, and he hit her again, and again, and again … and again.

I was so angry that tears ran down my face and heat rushed through my body. But then, somehow, my anger had reached a point where I actually became calm, sinister-like. Something had taken over me. I had reached my breaking point.

I went into my closet, pulled out my baseball bat, put on

my sneakers—while still in my pajamas—walked through the tall grass and opened the side door of Sadie's home.

I could hear Mrs. Coughlin crying as her husband lashed out at Sadie, and I heard Sadie whimper after each crack of the belt.

Still, I was calm.

I walked up the stairs and stood in front of Sadie's door. My hands that shook out of fear earlier were now ice cold and steady.

Mrs. Coughlin was at her husband's side begging for him to stop when she saw me. Her eyes widened. "What are you doing here?"

Mr. Coughlin stopped and began to turn around.

My arms rose up as if I was preparing for a pitch, and before he could completely turn around, I bashed him over the head with my bat. His body slammed to the ground and blood seeped from his head.

"Nicky! What did you do!" Mrs. Coughlin screamed.

I stood in silence, unable to process what I had just done. And then it all hit me and I began to weep, not for what I had just done, but because it took me this long.

Sadie stood in shock as Mrs. Coughlin ran downstairs to call 9-1-1. "They're going to take me away now," she wept.

I shook my head. "*No! No, Sadie!* No one is going to take you away. Put on your sneakers, quickly!"

When she put on her sneakers, I grabbed her by the hand

and lead her outside, and we ran to the center of the tall grass to our family bunker. Mr. Coughlin, in one of his manic episodes, had thought of the idea, and he worked on it day and night until it was "safe." Once the foundation was laid, it was a group effort between our families to fabricate it and fill it with everything that was essential to our survival. We even had survival bags specific to each person. Whenever there was a big storm, we'd all gather in it and waited it out.

But no storm was greater than this. This storm had been brewing for years and now Sadie and I were the ones that needed to survive, and those bags were our only hope. In them were at the very least a day's worth of canned foods, two bottles of water, and flashlights in the event that we needed to evacuate the bunker. And if, for any reason, help never came, those bags told who we were: they contained our identification—birth certificates, social security cards, etc. But I didn't plan on dying that day, nor did I plan on Sadie dying, either. We took our bags and ran over to my house.

"What are we doing, Nicky?" Sadie asked, repeatedly.

My mind was going a hundred miles per hour, so I ignored her.

"*Nicky*, what are we doing?"

"Do you trust me?" I asked, even though I didn't trust myself, and she nodded without hesitation. My darling put her life in my hands and never thought twice.

"Then get on," I told her, as I picked up my bike from the side of my house and directed her to get on the pegs.

"Where are we going?" she asked.

"To the sunset," I answered.

By this time, my parents had been on the porch outside wondering what was going on across the grass. They thought I was asleep in my room until my father spotted me from the corner of his eye riding off with Sadie.

"Nicholi? Nicholi!"

He ran after us, but I was too fast and the slope of the hill helped increase my speed. I knew they'd come looking for us—"they," meaning my parents and police—but where I was going no vehicle could enter.

The darkness of the woods helped us stay hidden, but it also made it difficult for me to see where I was going. I had to follow the path that I made earlier with nothing more than our flashlights, which I told Sadie to keep toward the ground only a few feet in front of me so that no one can spot the lights from a distance. After a long ride, we got off the bike and had to walk the rest.

"Where are we going?" Sadie continuously asked. I ignored her for a while because I wanted to show her rather than tell her. When we got closer, I stopped. *"Shhh. Listen."*

She became nervous. She thought I was warning her of an animal. *"Nicky ... what is it?"*

"Listen closely. Do you hear it?" I dropped the bike, and we walked out into the open where the train was passing.

Her shoulders slumped. "Okay … now what?"

"Now we can go into the sunset. This is our escape."

"But … it's dark out, Nicky."

"What I mean is, we can get on a train, and it will take us to where the sun *sets*."

She was apprehensive, and rightfully so. "Get on a train? How?"

"Remember when I told you that I watched the trains for hours?"

She nodded.

"I noticed something."

"What?"

"There's a bend out there"—I pointed in the distance—"that forces all of the trains to slow down almost to a full stop. Do you see it?"

She squinted, but she couldn't see anything through the dark of the night.

"That's where we get on," I said enthusiastically, placing my hand in hers. "Are you ready?"

"You and me?" she asked.

I pretended to fix my imaginary tie as if I was one of the gentlemen she so loved in the black-and-white films. "You and me, darling."

We were children. We didn't know what we were doing.

We didn't know the dangers of which we were about to embark. We walked for half a mile and waited for a train to pass. After some time, a train came along the bend and, as I had said, slowed to almost a complete stop.

"That one!" Sadie said, pointing to a boxcar that was open. It would mean that we'd be exposed to the conditions of the climate, but it was the only car of the train that we could enter, so we hoped into it.

When we got in, we laid our stomachs on the car's floor and breathed a sigh of relief as we watched the scenery of the mountains, rivers and countryside the train sped passed. We watched nature's beauty until our eyes could no longer stay open. Sadie fell asleep with her head on my shoulder, and I fell asleep with my head on her head.

A few hours later, the cold reality (literally) woke us up. The temperature had dropped drastically, and we woke up shivering. We were only wearing our pajamas, and the winds broke through the thin material with ease. We held each other tightly and rubbed each other's arms, but it didn't help. We were so cold that we could barely speak; we trembled from our lips to our toes.

"N-Nicky, l-look," Sadie said as her teeth chattered. She had noticed that toward the back of the crates, which was to the side of us, there were moving blankets covering more crates. We hadn't noticed them earlier because we were fixated on the scenery. We quickly untied one of them, pulled it off and covered ourselves. It not only gave us warmth, but it revealed something of equal necessity—*food*. Within the crates, underneath the rest of the blankets, was inventory for a supermarket—waters, juices, cereals, paper towels, soaps, you name it. A gift was given to us before we even knew we needed it. Sadie and I celebrated like the kids we were. We had everything that we needed to survive: warmth, food ... each other.

CHAPTER THREE

"Where did you go? You two couldn't have lived on that train forever."

"We rode the train for three days—two sunsets and three sunrises—until it reached its first and *final* stop."

I woke up to the screeching of the train's brakes, so I peeked out of the boxcar. I saw workers unloading the cars in front of ours. Frightened that they'd find us, I shook Sadie awake. We took the blanket, our survival bags, a box of cereal and half a gallon of water, and then we hopped out the side of the train and ran quickly to a wooded area. In a bush, we watched the workers unload.

"Damn it!" one worker said. "These damn animals got into the supply again. The boss is going to kill us!"

"I told you, you didn't shut that door completely. But *no*

you're Mr. I'm Always Right," said the other worker.

We giggled listening to them bicker.

"Hold on. You hear that?" one of them said.

"What?"

Sadie and I became completely quiet.

"Nothing. I ... I thought I heard kids."

"I told you to stop smoking that stuff."

"Working with you, it's a necessity, Alex."

Those two gentlemen were comedians and didn't even know it. They eventually moved on to the other boxcars after writing a report, and when they did, we made our escape down what seemed to be a never-ending road.

The "adventure" soon ran its course. No homes or people were anywhere to be found, and our only company was the sound of pebbles breaking with ever step we took to nowhere. We walked from dawn to dusk and still found no rest, and by then we had run out of water and food. Sadie leaned on me, and I on her, as we dragged ourselves with every step. Our throats felt like sandpaper, our feet were blistered, and our hope had withered away. This was no way for children to feel, but it was better than the alternative. I would have rather died with her outside like an animal than to know Sadie was being tortured as one. At least we were going through it together.

The moon began to show itself; the night was coming—

and with it, the cold. We had no choice but to stop, so Sadie and I put the blanket on the side of the road and wrapped ourselves in it. Lying there reminded me of when we were infants. Our parents used to show us pictures of us being swaddled together the same way we were in that blanket. I realized then, that before I've ever seen myself in the mirror—*before I ever saw my own reflection*—I looked into Sadie's eyes. Now here we were, swaddled once again under different circumstances. Sadie closed her eyes and I closed mine, and we planned to sleep together forever.

No car had driven down that road all day, but 10 minutes into sleep—10 minutes into giving up—we heard a car coming. Sadie and I peeked out of the blanket and then sat up quickly. When we did this, we saw a deer jump in front of the car, and the car skidded to the left in our direction. Its blaring lights became larger as it sped toward us. Sadie and I held each other tight, fearing the worst, but then the car braked. Smoke came up from its burnt tires, and the driver's door flew opened.

A woman, later to be known to us as Daji, came out with her hand over her mouth and rushed over to us. "What are you two doing out here!"

We remained quiet. We didn't know what to say or what to do.

"Come." She stuck out her hand. "I'll take you to your parents."

Instinctively, I stepped in front of Sadie and shook my head.

Daji pushed the subject. "Where do you live?"

"We're not from here," I answered.

"Then where?"

"Far away."

Disappointment fell upon her face. "So you two ran away, huh?"

I nodded.

"Do you not speak, young lady?" she asked, looking past me.

"Yes, ma'am," Sadie answered with a hoarse voice. She was so thirsty that it hurt to speak.

"It's dark, and there are animals of both beast and men out here …" Daji began to lecture us. As she spoke, I stepped back to Sadie's side and lifted her shirt just below her rib cage.

"We ran away from an animal," I said.

Daji's eyes widened, and once again, she placed her hand over her mouth.

Although Sadie's throat was dryer than a rock in a desert, she still had tears reserved for her pain, and they ran down like a fresh fountain. She wasn't only embarrassed, but terrified that Daji would send her back home.

Daji remained speechless, and she walked around in circles with her hands at her sides. "What am I supposed to do—leave you children out in the cold?" she rhetorically asked.

Sadie and I remained quiet.

"Get inside," she said, pointing to her car.

"We're not going back," I said sternly, shaking my head and grabbing Sadie's hand tight.

Daji's voice became softer and warm. "We can discuss this later. But first, let's get you two out of this cold and get some food in your bellies, okay?"

I looked at Sadie, and she agreed. If she had said no, I would have gladly lied back down in that blanket with her.

"LORD Jesus,"—Daji threw her hands up in the air as she walked us back to the car—"guide the way, GOD." She then got into the car, turned around to us, and with a smile, said, "We're going to figure this out. Don't you two worry, okay?"

She drove us to her home. Sadie and I got out of the car and stood cautiously at a distance.

"Come on, don't worry. I'm no more harm than you are to yourselves right now. Let's get you two cleaned up."

Although we were apprehensive, her voice was a voice that brought comfort to us, and somehow, we knew everything she spoke was true.

Life rushed back into Sadie's face when the warmth and scent of Daji's home surrounded us. Her home always smelled like food and dessert, so much so that it was just as much a part of her home's identity as the drapes on the windows and the paint on the wall. I can still smell that pecan cobbler today. *This* was the place we had dreamed of. *This* was our safe haven.

"Come," Daji said, escorting us to the kitchen. She took out two bottled waters from the fridge and gave it to us. We drank them in seconds. "Now sit," she said, pulling out two chairs from the table. She quickly fixed us something to eat from leftovers she had in the fridge, and all three of us sat together and ate. It felt right. It felt natural. It felt as if we had always been a family.

Daji barely touched her food because her stomach was too sick thinking about what we had been through, so she watched us eat. That was the quickest meal Sadie and I had ever put down, for two reasons: we were incredibly hungry, and as Daji would have liked to brag if you had met her in person, she was an incredible cook. When we finished eating, Daji took our plates, moved them to the side, and looked deep into our eyes. She stared at us for what felt like over a minute, clasped her hands and put her two index fingers on her lips. She then took a deep breath, leaned over the table and looked directly at Sadie and asked, "Who hurt you?"

Sadie got choked up and tried to hold her emotions in, but the build-up in her eyes told Daji all that she needed to know.

"*Look at me*, young lady," Daji said, as Sadie tried to look down to hide the tears that would inevitably fall. Sadie looked up with quivering lips. "Who hurt y—"

"Her dad. Her dad hurt her," I interrupted.

"Thank you, young man, but I need her to tell me. In order to get through the pain, sometimes you have to relive it."

Silence ruled the room. Sadie didn't know where to start.

Daji sighed. "I know it's hard."

Sadie looked over at me. I was the only one she had ever told her problems to. Trusting anyone else with her feelings was foreign to her.

"Look at *me*, young lady," Daji said again. "Do you know why I ask you this?"

Sadie shook her head.

"I ask you so that I can look into the eyes of someone familiar. Do you know who that is?"

Sadie shook her head again.

"Looking into your eyes is like looking into mine. I was once like you, in many ways."

"Like me?" Sadie asked. She never imagined someone would be able to relate to her.

Daji nodded. "How about I tell you my story and then you tell me yours? Is that fair?"

Sadie's eyes nervously wandered around the kitchen.

Daji brought her chair over, placed it between us and sat

down. "Is that fair?" she asked again.

Sadie took a deep breath and agreed.

My name is Diana Fawn.

I was once a young, happily married woman who, during that period of time, was right to believe that I would have a fairy-tale life. But then God decided to throw me a curve ball, and my body struck out time after time. God decided that He would make me barren.

My infertility was too much of a burden on my marriage and became the focal point of every fight—whether it was intended or not—and my husband and I fought day after day. While I always held out hope, my husband had given up. After numerous miscarriages, he grew cold toward me and began to neglect me as if I was no longer worthy of him. He had given up on children, he had given up on family ... he had given up on me. I found myself not only fighting for his attention but also his respect. The fighting soon became too much, and one day, my persistent arguing pushed him to his limit, so far that he retaliated in an unthinkable way. He slapped the words out of my mouth and swelled my lips shut, and that slap became the doorway to further abuse. From that day forward, if I even attempted to speak up, he would hurt me. He found power in my fear and used that power to replace the power that he had lost when he was told he would never be a father. There was a period in time when I couldn't remember a day without a bruise; I couldn't even remember what it was like to have soft, supple skin.

And you know what? I sought out help many times. I called the only family member I had. I called my sister, who had given me my nickname—Daji. I cried out to her more times than I can count, to the point where I could barely speak. Her advice was to forgive him and try to get some counseling in order to move forward. My flesh and bones, blood of my blood, skin of my skin, the one who shares my DNA, backed the beast who laid his paws on me. "Till death do you part," she reminded me. "For better or worse—you made those vows."

But I was a strong woman—like you are, young lady—and I ran away like you, but I was an adult while you are only a child. I ran away and drove to my sister's house and rang her doorbell in the middle of the night. I had fled from the beast and was waiting for my sister's arms to welcome me. My eyes shared the look that yours have today.

The door opened.

"Come in," my sister said.

I was a wreck, but I was content knowing that I was with her.

"Sit down," she insisted.

I took a deep breath and sat on the couch, my hands shaking.

My sister went upstairs. It was my assumption that she had gone to tell her husband. I couldn't make out exactly what she was saying.

She made her way back downstairs with her cell at her ear. "Uh huh, correct. No, it's not for me. It's for my sister. Her name? Diana Fawn. Yes, that's F-a-w-n, like dawn but with an F. No, she doesn't have any children. Yes, just her."

I smiled to myself. It was my thought that not only was my sister bringing me peace by allowing me to stay in her home, but justice by calling the police. She had not only come to my aide, she wanted the beast to be chained and locked away.

"You mean, she can't come today?" my sister sighed. "Well, okay then, tomorrow will do. Thank you for the information. I will let her know." My sister jotted down the information she was given on a piece of paper, hung up the phone and handed it to me.

"What's this?" I asked.

"That's the phone number to a woman's shelter. They will have a room for you tomorrow afternoon."

My heart skipped a beat. "A what?"

My sister had a clueless look on her face. "A woman's shelter," she repeated.

My body had suddenly forgotten what it meant to take in air and my mouth forgot what words were.

"Oh, Daji, you know I'd love to have you—I really would," she said, her voice trailing off while her eyes spoke the truth: I was a burden. "There's just no room. I'm about to have my son and the only room available is his nursery, which of course he'll need. You know if I had the space I would gladly take you

in."

I looked around myself, peeked over at the family room just across from me and then at the couch that I was sitting on.

"No room?" I asked. It was hard enough for me to ring that bell and ask for help. Now my worst nightmare had come try. I had extended my hands in hope that they would be held, and they were slapped down.

"Oh, honey, please don't cry. I'm pregnant. You're going to get me all emotional. You have to be strong, okay? Momma raised us to be strong women. You're going to be fine. The worst part is over. You got out of there," she said.

She had no idea how much more her rejection hurt. I'd rather be strangled to my last breath than to feel unwanted by the one person who should have begged me to stay.

"You know I love you," she dared to say. That wasn't love. I've loved dogs more than she loved me. And that's how I felt—like a dog.

I didn't argue with her. I remained silent and composed. She was right about one thing—Momma raised us to be strong. To be honest, somewhere inside of me I was wishing it was all a joke. I was waiting for her to burst out in laughter, telling me how silly I was to think she would ever say such things. But that uncontrollable laughter between two close sisters never came, so I got up and showed myself out.

"Where are you going?" she asked.

At first, I ignored her and continued to walk, but then I

stopped. I knew that would be the last time I would ever see my sister—there was no turning back from that betrayal—so I had to say my goodbye. I walked back and kneeled at her feet. I put my hands on my sister's stomach, looked up at her and said, "I pray that one day, when your child becomes a man and has siblings, that he does not treat them the way his mother has treated me." I then kissed her stomach, got up on my two feet and walked to my car. I drove far away, without any idea as to where I was going. I just drove as far as I could—from the darkness of the morning to the darkness of the night, from the heat of one state to the chill of another. I drove as if there was a destination that would bring me answers as to why some people can be so cruel. Yet, to this day, I am still seeking those answers.

I had made many stops during my cross-country trip, but one particular stop changed my life. I needed to fill up the tank, as I had done many times without any interruption, so I pulled into a gas station. I got some food, hygiene products to clean myself up in the public bathroom and requested the clerk to fill up my tank. But when I went to pay with my credit card, it was declined. I called the bank, and they told me that my husband had requested that they stop all further charges on my card because, in his words, "there had been some recent fraudulent purchases." He had cancelled my card out of spite, hoping that I'd come crawling back to him. And then, within minutes after hanging up the phone with the bank, two police cars pulled up to the station. They walked inside, and I could hear the dispatcher over their radios.

"Possible stolen vehicle in the area."

My heart sank.

Could my husband have gone so low to report our car stolen? I thought to myself.

"Four-door sedan, blue paint job, license plate number 5LKC534."

I breathed a sigh of relief.

"Ma'am, that'll be seventy-seven dollars and seven cents," the clerk said. I had forgotten, for a moment, about making payment. I apologized to the clerk, left everything I was going to purchase on the counter and quickly made my way back to the car.

I sat in my car, staring at the fuel gauge; its arrow nearly on empty. My car was the one thing I thought I could rely on, and now even it had given up on me. I had no money, no gas … no place to go. And to make things worse, the temperature was dropping. I had no other choice but to keep driving, and I did just that. I drove as far as I could until my car came to a screeching halt. I made it a mile and a half from the gas station. I was now sitting in my car, hungry and cold. No one was going to come and rescue me. Perhaps no one would find me either, I thought. And although this may be hard to comprehend, being that you will find a crucifix in every room of this home, I wasn't much of a religious person back then.

But in that moment, I had found myself parked across from a church and was more desperate than I had ever been. So rather than continue to be a skeptic, I prayed—and I prayed so long that I fell asleep from exhaustion.

My eyes would open in the early morning the next day to the sound of the church's bells. And although droves of people walked out of the small church—some even walking past my car—I felt like I was the only person in the world. I felt forgotten. I felt so isolated and distant as I watched families bond with each other. I had no family and no way of creating one. God had made me barren, and the only family I ever knew had either beaten or neglected me. I felt like a mistake. I felt like God had decided to discard me. Deep in my misery, I suddenly became hot and claustrophobic in the car, so I stepped out to get some air. I tried to breathe, but every time I tried I felt like I wasn't taking in enough air. With every breath I took, rather than expand, my chest became tighter. Everyone around me noticed my struggle and stared with concern. "Excuse me, are you okay?" one woman (Maryanne) asked. It felt like everyone was encircling me, and I became even more claustrophobic. "Are you okay?" she asked again. My hands and feet were cold to the touch and were becoming numb. I tried to squeeze my hands together to get the blood flowing, but it didn't help. This wasn't like me. I was beginning to feel like my soul was somehow outside of my body.

"Someone get her a chair!" Maryanne shouted.

I saw a gentleman running toward me with a folding chair and then everything went black; I had collapsed into Maryanne's arms. She held me and never let go. A few seconds later, I gained consciousness and opened my eyes, but what I had feared so much had now become reality—I could not move my body. Every motor skill was shutting down. My family had neglected me, God (I thought) had neglected me, my car had neglected me, and now my body had neglected me. I felt like a lost soul—no one, nothing, and not even my own body wanted a part of me.

Maryanne could only hold me for so long, so the gentleman that had gone into the church to get me a chair kindly took her place and lifted me into his arms. He brought me into the church, where it was warm and smelled like baked goods, and placed me down into another chair, holding me up gently by my shoulders.

"Can you hear me?" Maryanne asked, snapping her fingers in front of my eyes.

I stared blankly at her.

She looked over at the gentleman, concerned. "I think we're going to need to call an ambulance."

Just like that, in an instant, I snapped out of my shock and grabbed on to her hand. I shook my head frantically, fearing that my husband may find me, and tears rolled down my cheeks.

Maryanne placed her hand over mine—her touch was so

gentle—and asked the gentleman to get a cup of water and another chair. He kindly did so, and she sat in front me and watched me drink. I exhaled and my teeth chattered as if my nerves were shocked back into life. Her hand, again, gently touched mine, and made me calm when all I wanted to do was run away to an unknown destination—to run away from everything … even myself.

"Julius," she said, looking at the gentleman. "Give us a moment to talk, will you?" He nodded and closed the door behind him.

We talked for hours, and she not once looked as if she was disinterested. She genuinely cared for me—a complete stranger. During this long talk, I asked if Maryanne knew anyone that might want to buy my car as a means of earning some cash to find a place to sleep and get some food. Maryanne refused to allow it. Instead, she offered me a room in the church itself and the food that was stored in its pantry. The only condition was that I attend Bible study every Wednesday, clean up the church daily, and watch the children in the church's daycare while the adults had Bible study on Sunday. Watching children was my specialty. I was a 5th grade teacher for many years in my old town. It actually pained me to think about all the innocent, kind children I had left behind.

"Are you sure the pastor will allow this?" I asked, surprised by her generosity and authority over all that she had mentioned. "He hasn't even met me."

*"**She** has told you that you could, and she's a woman of her word," Maryanne answered, with a smile.*

I was given a new start at life from a complete stranger who chose to love me more than the one who shares my blood and the one who I had put my entire life in the hands of. And after three months of intense job search and being able to rely on the kindness of the church—which had become not only a supportive community, but my new family—I finally landed a teaching job at the town's elementary school through a recommendation from a fellow brother of the church.

I had become a 5th grade teacher again.

Alleluia: GOD be praised!

Daji's eyes built up as she thought about how far she had come. She then got up from her chair and walked over to the sink. Her back was turned to us, hands on the sink's edge.

"What am I to do, children?"

Neither Sadie nor I could answer her.

"If I call child services, they will either send you back home or put you in foster care—both of which are lives you don't deserve. I see what those poor foster children have to go through every day at school. I can easily pick them out of the crowd. Do you know how? They're the ones with lost hope. They're the ones with frowns where smiles should be." Daji took a moment to contain herself.

"They carry a burden no time can heal. I see hope missing in their eyes that I wish to *God* I could give them. I think about them every day. It is an awful thought to know that the innocence of a child has been taken away. And now, here you are, with that *same* pain in your eyes." Daji was overwhelmed; her breathing became heavy. "What do I do with you two? If I take you in and anyone finds out, they will crucify me. They will call me a kidnapper, lock me in a cell and throw away the key." She put her hand on the back of her neck, turned around, took a deep breath and made her way back to the table. She then moved the chair that was between Sadie and me, and kneeled down to our level. Again, silence ruled the room as she looked into our eyes. "But that's a risk I'm willing to take," she said.

Sadie and I looked at each other in disbelief.

"Look at me, honey," Daji said to Sadie, grabbing her tiny hand. "Whoever hurt you, will *never* hurt you again. Over my dead body will I allow that to happen. Do you hear me?" She then got up and took a step back so that both of us were in her sight. "You will be like my very own. I will take you in as my children, if …" she paused, and we stared up at her, her eyes burning into ours, her love radiating. "If … you would take me in as your mother."

That night Sadie and I found a mother in a stranger, just as Daji found a sister in Maryanne.

CHAPTER FOUR

"Sweet poetry!"

"Poetry?"

"Yes. Don't you see the poetic nature of life?"

"The what?"

"*Everything*—the good, the bad—happens for a reason. Daji was unable to have children, Sadie needed a parent, and you ..."

"I what?"

"*You needed a hero*. Although you three were in pieces, collectively you became whole. You became a *family*."

"I wish we were enough ..."

"Enough?"

"I wish we were enough for Sadie."

∞

Daji took care of us for seven years, and those were some of the best years of our lives—even though Sadie and I were confined most of the time to within the house. If ever we went outside, it was to the backyard because it was fenced off, and we would only go out when the neighbors went to work. Daji wasn't one who believed in fences—she *loved* people—but she put them up for us, for our comfort, for our sanity. Before she rescued us, she threw summer barbeques for the entire block and routinely had friends over for Sunday brunch. She was the neighborhood friend, sister, and counselor—but we needed a *mother* and we needed that fence. So she put up a divide, in more ways than one: she placed a divide between herself and all of those who she cared for so dearly—her neighbors, her brothers and sisters of the church, and even Maryanne— for the sake of keeping us safe. She took in two children and gave us a chance at life; she paid a debt that wasn't her own. She tended to us like the tender mother Sadie had always wished for and the hero that I needed. And she not only freed us from the beast that preyed on Sadie, she freed us from the beast of society—the beast that preys on the uneducated and the ones that don't get to start with a full deck of cards in this game called life. She wanted more for us than to simply survive—she wanted us to *thrive*. So not only did she prepare breakfast, lunch and dinner *every single day*, she also homeschooled us when she returned from work. She went above and beyond, and then some. Sure, it was certainly hard to be isolated from the public—especially as children—but in the end, it was her unconditional love and care that gave us *true* freedom.

That freedom came six years later, when Sadie and I turned eighteen. Eighteen meant that we were officially adults in the eyes of the state, which meant that if anyone was alerted that we were out roaming the world, there was nothing the state, government, police, our biological parents or any other authority could do to force us back "home." Eighteen meant physical freedom, but real freedom only comes when you have choices, and it was because of Daji's homeschooling we had those choices. She gave us a chance to go to college by providing us with the education we needed in order to take the test to get our GED, also known as the General Education Diploma. If we passed, it meant we'd have our full deck of cards.

We passed with flying colors.

When we finally went off to college, Daji had three requests: come back home for the holidays, call when we can, and never separate from each other. We abided by those requests, even down to our living situation in college. Rather than be separated in dorms because of the school's policy that boys and girls needed to have separate living quarters, Sadie and I rented a small apartment on the second floor of a private home. We worked after classes in order to pay for it and did numerous tasks for the home-owner in order to supplement for the low monthly rent. It was hard. It took its toll on us. But it was worth it. We kept our promise—we never separated. As for our education, Sadie went into psychology while I took general classes. I took general classes because I thought that I didn't know what I wanted to be, but looking back, I now realize that I didn't know what I wanted to do with my life because my focus wasn't on *my* life, it was on her. Deep down, I was troubled knowing she wanted to study psychology. I was troubled because I knew what she was seeking—she was seeking answers to allow herself to forgive him. Although it had been years, Mr. Coughlin still weighed heavily on her heart. Sadie was a star student driven solely by the hope of getting answers to why he had abused her.

In my heart, I always wanted to tell her to let them go, but I could never get the words out. I reasoned that everyone deserved to pursue not only happiness, but also peace. So I watched her obsess over her research like a mad scientist on the verge of a new breakthrough. I watched her eyes light up night after night as she read her textbooks. Her peers viewed her as an overachiever while I knew she was just a tortured soul. She viewed the world and all of its troubles as an opportunity to improve and learn while I had known the truth: you can only save those who wish to be saved. Indeed, I was cynical, but I was *right*.

I'd kept quiet for three and a half years until one day I had no choice but to tell her how I felt. She had given me no other option. I had protected her from hell, and she wanted to dive right back in.

One of the worst days of my life began with Sadie saying I love you. She whispered it so delicately as she stroked my hair while I slept. I woke up to her eyes fixed on me as if it was the last time she'd ever see me. I smiled, stretched out my arms and feet, and as I cleared my eyes, I saw her somber gaze.

"What's wrong?" I asked.

"I had a dream," she said, with a smile that held back sorrow.

"A nightmare?"

She shook her head. "No. It was beautiful."

"What was it about?"

"It was nighttime. You were sitting on a bench in a park. You cried, you laughed … you talked to me."

"What did I say?"

"It's not what you said. It's how you said it. You spoke as if I wasn't there, yet you were talking to me. I was beside you, yet I felt so far away."

"It was just a dream," I said, as I touched her to console

her. "You'll never be too far away. I'm going to be right here with you forever."

"Forever?"

"When there are no more stars in the sky or matter in the universe, there will still be our love."

She needed that assurance because she knew I would refuse what she was about to ask: "Wouldn't it be nice to go away, Nicky?"

"Sure."

"Wouldn't it be nice to go where it's hot, where the sun will finally shine back on our faces as it did when we were young and the grass is no longer cut, but left to grow wild?"

The details of her ideal vacation went right over my head. "That sounds nice. We do have the money saved up to go away during the winter break in two weeks. Where exactly do you want to go?"

She became quiet. She had hoped that I'd figure it out without having to say it.

I didn't understand her silence, so I asked again. "Where do you want—"

"I want to go home," she let out, with a gasp as if the air in her lungs were dying to escape.

Again, her request flew over my head. "Home? That's not a vacation. We go back home every break."

"No. I want to go *home*."

It finally sank in.

"I want to see my parents—my *real* parents."

I shook my head, not willing to accept it, and responded harshly. "That's not happening."

I knew I shouldn't have spoken so matter-of-factly, but my worst nightmare was returning to that dreadful place.

"*Are you insane?*" I continued. "Why would you want to go back there?"

She remained quiet, and I immediately felt terrible about how I had spoken.

"I … I just don't want you to get hurt, Sadie."

"I need to go back, Nicky. I can help him—*I know I can.* If I don't do this, I'll go crazy. *I have to try.*"

"What if he doesn't even open the door for you? Will you be okay with that? Will you move on then?"

"My mother will. I know she will."

"The woman who allowed you to be abused is now going to help you?"

"People change, Nicholi."

"What if they didn't, then what?"

"Then I'd at least have closure in knowing that I tried."

"Closure? That chapter of your life has been closed for many years. Your story is different now. *Our* story is different now. We tore out those pages long ago."

"It'll kill me if I don't try. *It'll eat me whole, Nicholi.* I now understand where his pain is coming from, and why my mother stood by his side. He can't forgive himself for what he's done in the war. He can't find peace knowing he lives in a world full of chaos, and she can't help but love the man that's within the darkness—and neither can I. I have to go, with or without you. *I must.* I will see to it that they climb out of the hell they've come to live in. If I don't, then who will? What kind of daughter would I be if I don't try?

"What kind of daughter would you be? I can't believe my ears. Do you think you're a bad daughter because you ran away? *You're not!* You're a *survivor.* You weren't wrong for leaving. He could've beaten you to death, both you *and* your mother. Who knows if he hasn't alre—"

"Stop. *Please* ... stop, Nicky." She trembled beneath her skin from the very thought and got up to walk in circles.

I had gone too far.

"I'm going, Nicholi. I've made my decision and that's that."

I could see that she was on the verge of breaking down, so I decided to stay quiet and just listen to her even though my gut turned inside out.

"Isn't this what love is after all?" she continued. "Love isn't easy, Nicholi. Sometimes we have to forgive and show mercy and compassion to those who may not deserve it. Someone's got to do it, and I'll be damned if I'm not that person. I'm their *flesh and blood.*" She paused for a moment, breathing deeply. "They weren't always this way, you know? They were once as we are. They were madly in love, and I'm the physical proof of that. *I exist because of them.*"

I could no longer remain quiet. "You're wrong. They're not like us. We've been through too much to be compared."

"You've protected me since we were children, Nicholi, and I understand that that is what you are still trying to do. But I'm a grown woman now, and I need to make my own decisions. Please understand that I need to do this for myself."

Rather than accept it, I, regrettably, flipped the argument. "What about me? What do I do?"

"There's nothing for you to do. This is something that *I* need to do."

"I can't let you go back there by yourself, so what does that mean for me? I'll tell you. It means that I have to see my parents, too." My blood pressure rose, and I paced back and forth. "What am I supposed to do now? Do I just knock on their door and pretend none of this happened? Explain how this works, Sadie! This wasn't a temporary escape. It was supposed to be *forever*."

"You forgive. That's what you do," she wisely responded, knowing my argument for going back home wasn't out of fear of explaining to them why I had left, but out of anger toward them. "You try to understand their point of view and then you forgive, no matter what."

"Their point of view? A little girl was hurt day after

day—the proof was right in front of their eyes—yet they took no action. Could you forgive me if I did that? Would you be able to look at me the same way if I turned a blind eye to someone in need, especially a child?"

She stood in silence, knowing she couldn't. She had held me to a different standard. In that moment, she knew that she had lost the argument, so she walked toward the window and looked out. I could see that she was looking at her dream float away as if it was being carried by the wind.

It broke my heart, so I caved in.

"Fine. We'll go back," I said. I would regret those words forever. It was the worst mistake of my life.

"Really!" she shouted in excitement. "You'd do that for me?"

Although I was looking into her eyes, I could clearly see that her heart was full. Any reason that I would've had to reconsider was shut out by her joy.

CHAPTER FIVE

"What's wrong, Nicholi? Why'd you stop?"

"You ... you said life is poetic."

"Yes. I did."

"What about death?"

"What about it?"

"Will GOD bring me back to my Sadie? Is death as poetic as life?"

"I think you know, Nicholi. Love never dies."

"Mine has."

"Are you sure you want to do this?" I asked, as we were now parked in my parents' driveway, and Sadie nodded without hesitation. I took the keys out of the ignition, stepped out and made my way up to the front door. I was flooded with emotions as I thought about the past, so I needed a moment to gather myself.

When I finally went to knock, the door flew open and out came my mother. Her face was pale and her eyes shed tears that seemed like they would never end. I didn't say anything, but I welcomed her embrace. She hugged me so tight that I thought she might leave a permanent mark on my arms and back.

My father stood in shock behind her and leaned on the piano in the foyer to hold himself up. He couldn't believe his eyes as he stared at his boy who now resembled him.

Still, I had nothing to say. I wasn't there for them. I wasn't there for me. I was there for Sadie.

I turned around and signaled her to come out.

I didn't think my mother had any more tears left in the ducts of her eyes, but they flowed even more when she saw Sadie.

My father slowly made his way over to us, struggling with each step. He was a man who rarely showed his emotions, but for the first time, he was defenseless. When he saw Sadie step out of the car, he took a deep breath and a tear fell upon his cheek.

My parents repeatedly expressed their sorrow to Sadie and I. And rather than appreciate what they were saying, I grew angrier the more I heard it; their apologies were a reminder of the unnecessary life Sadie had to overcome because they simply refused to act. Two *children* had to be brave while the adults closed their doors and shut their windows to a child who needed them. And in this way, through their silence, they contributed to her abuse.

All of that anger almost poured out of me, but Sadie showed me I was wrong with a gentle touch on my back as she walked past me to embrace my parents. She could've stood in the car and turned her back to them just as they did to her, but she chose to forgive because *that* was who she was.

"Please come inside," my mother said, nearly begging.

Sadie stepped forward first and held my hand as we followed my parents inside. This place I once called home had now felt foreign to me.

"Please sit down," my mother insisted, pointing to the couch. And we did. In fact, we sat in the living room for hours talking to my parents. They asked us many questions, like where did we go, who raised us and how we were doing. I remember drowning out their voices, like the music that's played in an elevator, as I watched Sadie so patiently and kindly feed them generic answers to every question they had. I was in awe watching how effortlessly she did it because I knew how she was *really* feeling. Even though she conversed flawlessly, her eyes would look up at the clock here and there, and in those microseconds, her façade collapsed. In those discreet glances, behind fronted smile, Sadie's eyes showed her desperate hope of being welcomed as warmly by Mr. and Mrs. Coughlin as my parents had welcomed her.

"Well,"—I broke my parents never-ending questions—"it's time Sadie and I got going. We have to go see the Coughlins. She wants to mend their relationship."

The keyword was *she*.

"I wish you'd stay, Nicky. I was just about to make supper," my mother said.

"No, thank—"

Sadie tapped me on my thigh. "Sure. We'd love to eat dinner. And if you don't mind, we'd like to stay the night, too."

I shook my head.

"It's okay, Nicholi. It's probably best that I get some rest after the long trip, anyway. Tomorrow will come soon enough. We'll spend the night here and then tomorrow morning I'll head over to see my parents."

"Fine. We'll stay the night, but tomorrow—" I placed my hand on top of hers "—*we* are going to your parents."

Sadie knew there was no way of convincing me to let her go alone, so she changed the subject and turned her attention back to my mother. "Can you show us where we would sleep tonight?"

"You can stay in Nicky's room. I haven't changed a thing."

"You haven't changed anything?" I asked, as we all made

our way up the stairs.

"Your mother always had hope that you'd come back home, Nicky," my father answered.

"Welcome back," my mother said, opening the door to my room.

I felt as if I was sent back in time, and I became that little boy again standing by the windowsill hoping Sadie was okay. I grabbed Sadie's hand, and I didn't need to speak for her to understand what I was saying when I looked at her. She knew no one was going to hurt her ever again.

She rested her head on my shoulder and stared at her home through my window.

"We'll leave you two alone for now," my mother said, closing the door behind her. I appreciated that. I knew how much she wanted to spend every second with me. For once, she wasn't selfish.

"We could go back home if you want," I told Sadie.

She didn't speak, but she shook her head lightly as her eyes remained glued to her old home.

We barely slept that night, but the few times Sadie did fall asleep, she jumped up almost immediately because she was filled with so much anxiety. The night had felt like forever for her, but the morning came too soon for me. I had a knot in my stomach. I knew something was wrong, but I dismissed my gut. While I felt sick, Sadie was elated. She told me that she had seen Mr. and Mrs. Coughlin from my window earlier in the morning while I was asleep. She had seen them come out of their home and drive off together. She talked about how she saw great love between them. She told me how much they laughed and couldn't keep their hands off each other—they were like high school kids all over again. She kept repeating how Mr. Coughlin had to have changed because this wasn't a side of him she'd ever seen.

Since Sadie's parents had left earlier that morning, we spent the day with my parents. But when the clock struck six, Sadie decided that it was time to go see if Mr. and Mrs. Coughlin had returned. It was time to walk my darling back into hell.

Sadie hugged my parents, thanked them for their hospitality and promised to return soon. We then went through the tall grass.

My heart was pounding. I was terrified to see Mr. and Mrs. Coughlin, not for what they would do or say, but for what I might. I was *literally* biting my tongue. Because of this, I had to stop before making it out of the tall grass. Sadie asked me what was wrong, and I couldn't lie. I told her I was scared of ruining her opportunity with them. I didn't think I could control myself. My nerves were shooting through my body as I remembered what they had done to her. I made the decision right there that I would stay within the grass and allow Sadie to reconcile with her family, alone. So she went, and I looked on.

Mrs. Coughlin was hanging clothes in the yard. It seemed like the clock had turned back time because she looked better than ever. She looked like she could have been Sadie's older sister.

Sadie walked toward her mother quietly and kept looking back at me, like a child uncertain of what to do.

Mrs. Coughlin was singing, humming and carrying on as she hung up her bright-colored clothes in the blazing heat.

"Mom ..." Sadie spoke softly.

Mrs. Coughlin, without turning around, stood in shock and dropped the blouse that was in her hand. She turned her ear halfway over her shoulder and took a deep breath.

Sadie spoke again, "Mom, it's—"

"Sadie?" Mrs. Coughlin asked, turning around to face her daughter.

Sadie was at a loss for words and simply nodded.

Unable to believe her own eyes, Mrs. Coughlin walked up to her, touched her face and the beauty mark on her head. She then fell to her knees in a way of asking for forgiveness.

Sadie could not act in the same manner as she did with my parents. She had no words. She just stood there and allowed her mother to embrace her legs. She needed me the way I needed her. I couldn't leave my darling alone, not in a moment like this.

"Mrs. Coughlin," I spoke up, making my way out of the tall grass.

Her head turned swiftly to the right. "Nicky? Is that you, too?"

I, mindfully, held my tongue. It was hard not to say the things I had been thinking most of my life, but all I had to do was look at Sadie.

"Yes. It's me, Mrs. Coughlin."

She got up, made her way over to me and gave me a hug that competed with my mother's. *"Thank you,"* she said.

I could no longer hold my tongue and asked her a loaded question: "For what?"

She understood my words from my tone, so she let go of me and put her face to the ground.

"Nicholi," Sadie scolded me.

I gritted my teeth. "Mrs. Coughlin ... it was Sadie's decision to come back and see you. You should know that not a day has gone by that she hasn't thought about you. I know it's hard for her to find the words right now, but she loves you."

Mrs. Coughlin closed her eyes, took a deep breath and then walked back to Sadie. She held my darling's hands and began to say the words that Sadie had always wished she had. "You are my daughter, blood of my blood, flesh of my flesh. I should've protected you. I'm so sorry for what happened to you. *I'm so, so sorry.*"

Sadie choked up.

Mrs. Coughlin continued, "There are some things that you should know."

"It's okay, Momma," Sadie interrupted; she didn't want to head down that dark road. "I've come back to forgive you and Papa. I want the past to be the past."

Sadie made a mistake right there and then. She should have let her mother tell her.

"Where's Papa?"

"Anthony went out to town."

"Where?"

"To a bar."

Sadie was disappointed in hearing this. "He's still drinking?"

Mrs. Coughlin, as usual, found a way to justify his behavior. "Not as often as before, just on the weekends. Everyone deserves their own time. This is how he spends his."

Although she was protecting his ways, she was right. He *was* a different man. He didn't drink as much as he used to and he no longer had his fits of rage—because he no longer had reason to. Sadie was gone. She was out of sight and out of mind. He could *breathe* again.

"When will he be back?"

"Tonight."

"Okay. We'll wait for him."

Fear came over Mrs. Coughlin and she began to stammer, "Well, um, maybe ... maybe you should come back another time."

"Another time? *It's been a decade.*"

Mrs. Coughlin scrambled for an excuse. "Sadie, honey, you know Anthony doesn't like surprises."

"But I'm his daughter."

Mrs. Coughlin looked away and stood in silence. I could see the battle in her eyes. She knew that her husband would not be happy seeing Sadie, but Sadie didn't let up. She fought tooth and nail.

"It's been too long."

"Please, honey, can you give me some time? I promise you, this is the best way. Let me speak to him *first*."

I took Sadie by the arm and turned her to me. "I know this isn't the way you had planned, but your mother is right. You know the last thing I want to do is agree with her, but I do. Give her some time to speak with him."

She was hurt and on the verge of tears, but she shook them off and agreed. "Fine. I'll come back tomorrow."

"Come the following day. Anthony, he ... well, sometimes he doesn't feel too good the day after."

Sadie wanted to scream, but held it in.

"Everything is going to be fine, honey," Mrs. Coughlin assured her, placing her hands on Sadie's cheeks and intentionally kissing the beauty mark on her head.

"*Two days, Mama.* No more than that, okay?"

"Two days, honey."

After their agreement, Sadie and I went back to my family's home and we sat on the porch, just as we had when we were children. She laid her head on my shoulder and we sat in silence for a while.

I contemplated whether I should ask her there, but then I thought of a better place. "Come with me," I told her, grabbing her hand.

"Where?"

"Just follow."

Her curiosity took the place of her angst, and after walking for a few minutes, she knew where we were going.

"Nicholi, *I know where you're taking me.*"

I smiled and continued to walk with her hand in mine. Throughout the entire time of our walk, I had never let go of her hand, and when we arrived, I turned to her and grabbed the other.

"Why are we here, Nicky?" Sadie asked as we stood beside the train tracks.

"It was here that we took a leap of faith. It was here that we entrusted each other with our lives and never looked back." I got down on one knee and took the ring out from my pocket. She put her hand over her mouth and her eyes gleamed with love. "Will you take another leap of faith with me?"

She got down on her knees so that her eyes met mine,

and shook her head. "This isn't a leap. I never planned on *anything* else. I married you when we jumped on that train a decade ago. And I'll marry you again, a hundred times—a thousand times. *I could never marry you enough*."

I kissed my darling then, and it felt like God himself had joined us in that moment. It felt like He had sewn my soul to hers. And in a show of symbolic confirmation of our unity, a freight train sped past us.

We went back to my parents' home soon after and shared the news. Sadie, as many newly engaged women do, showed off her ring. My mother was ecstatic, my father gave me a cigar—the joy in that room was true bliss. I wish I could've frozen that moment in time and cast away the future, but the future could not be held back because it seeded itself in Sadie's hope for reuniting with her family. Even during that euphoric celebration I, once again, caught her helplessly glancing up at the clock. My sweet Sadie … all she wanted was to experience that same joy with her family, too.

It was 11:30 that night when lightning ripped through the sky and its thunder rang as if it was hitting solid rock. I tried to convince Sadie to get some rest, but she refused. She chose to sit on my windowsill and stare at her child-hood home in the distance. I fell asleep watching her. I should have stayed awake. I should have talked to her more. I should have held her. I should've known what she was waiting up for …

Around two in the morning, Sadie made her grave mistake. She had seen Mr. Coughlin pull up in his car, and reacted. Her anxiousness got the best of her.

I had slept through the crashing thunder of the night, yet awoke to the creaking of my bedroom door. Before I could clear my bleary eyes, I heard Sadie run downstairs and exit the house. I stuck my head out of the window and saw her running through the tall grass.

I quickly put on my sneakers and ran after her, and when I caught up, I saw her knocking on every surface of the house—the panels, the windows, the doors—calling out for him, "Papa! Open the door! It's me!"

I ran over to her, grabbed her by the arm and dragged her away from the house. She kept shoving me, trying her best to free herself. I'd never seen that side of her before. It's as if she was temporarily mad. It hurt me to pull her away so forcefully, but I did it with good reason.

I almost made it back into the tall grass with her, but it was too late. The damage had been done. She caught the attention of the beast.

Mr. Coughlin kicked open his door and let off a gunshot into the air, which was hidden by the surrounding thunder.

It was pitch dark where Sadie and I were standing, so he turned on the porch light and angled it at us.

"Who's out there!" he yelled out.

I knew Mr. Coughlin was drunk by his slurred words.

Mrs. Coughlin came running out. "Anthony! Put down the gun. That's ... that's Sadie."

"Papa, it's *me*. I came back home."

Mr. Coughlin spit out his tobacco and walked to the end of the porch. "What did you call me?"

The rain began to come down heavier, and we were drenched from head to toe. Sadie, wiping her face, said once more, "It's *me*, Papa."

Mr. Coughlin turned to his wife and then looked back at Sadie; his eyes squinted in disbelief.

Believing that Mr. Coughlin had a hard time seeing her through the heavy rain, Sadie made her way over to the porch and stood in front of him.

It took a lot for me to stay back, but I did. I knew I would only make matters worse.

Mr. Coughlin analyzed her face—up, down, side to side.

"You look like your mother," he said.

"I'm sure you're somewhere in here, too," she responded.

Mr. Coughlin took a step closer to her and spit his tobacco at her side. "There's nothing of me in you."

Seeing Mr. Coughlin so close to Sadie gave me a pit in my stomach. I was terrified that he'd turn back to his old ways, so I dug my feet into the mud to gain traction in case

I needed to run at him.

"Sure there is, Papa," she said, placing her hand on his left arm. He didn't like that at all. The moment she placed her hand on his arm, he placed his gun on her chest.

"Anthony!" I yelled out. I kept shouting his name and waving my hands to distract him. "Anthony!"

That was a mistake, a mistake that would haunt me forever. Why did I call him by his first name? All of my days as a child I called him by his title. Perhaps if I had done so, he would have known it was me, but he was so drunk that he thought I was someone else.

He shoved Sadie to the side and made his way down the stairs and into the rain to meet me.

"You were my friend, Jimmy!" he cried out as he now pointed his gun at me. "You were my *best friend. Why'd you do it?*"

Sadie quickly got up, ran down the stairs and stood in front of him. "Papa!" she called out to him, as if he was lost and all he needed to do was listen to her voice. "Put the gun—" Before she could say anymore, he slapped her, and she fell to the ground.

She should've let him shoot me. I would've gladly taken that fate over the one that was to come.

Mr. Coughlin kept his gun aimed at me to ensure that I wouldn't make a move and then he grabbed Sadie by her hair.

"Let her go!" I warned, fearlessly walking toward him.

He let out a shot to my side into the grass, and the thick mud splashed on my leg. He knew he had the upper hand and smirked as if he was playing a game of chess. I had no moves and he had many. He made the next move: he tightened his grip around Sadie's hair, and she groaned. I could see the veins bulging in her neck.

"You took my wife, Jimmy!" Mr. Coughlin cried out.

I was utterly confused.

"You took everything from me! Look what you did!" Mr. Coughlin continued, as he tossed Sadie in front of him like an unwanted animal. His tone then became more sadistic. "I should have done this years ago. I'm going to take from you the way you took from me!"

Sadie struggled to get up. Her strained neck made it hard for her to gain balance, so she began to crawl to me. I couldn't move to help her because Mr. Coughlin still had his gun locked on me, so I was forced to stay put and witness my darling desperately crawl through the mud like an injured dog. She eventually managed to get up—to Mr. Coughlin's surprise—and when she did, she ran to me.

I think about that moment every day of my life. I can still feel the rain on my skin, the frigid temperature of the night, every single breath I took ... and every step in Sadie's stride. One more yard. All she needed was *three more steps*. She was *so* close.

As Sadie reached out for me, Mr. Coughlin shot her twice in the back, and she fell into my arms. I immediately turned my back toward him to shield her, and he let off two more. He hit me in my right rib and hip, and I fell to the ground, and she to my side.

My right lung collapsed, and the heavy rain pounded down my throat—I was simultaneously suffocating and drowning. But even then, my fear was not of death; I only feared being without Sadie. Whether it was I that went before her or she before me, the agony of being without her for even a second was worse than death itself.

It was frightening to hear myself gasping for air, but no more horrific than hearing my darling gurgling her own blood.

Life was fading from her eyes quickly, and she stretched out her hand for me. It was impossible to move, but I managed to place my hand in hers, and when I did, I could feel our pulses slowing together. For a moment, it was beautiful: we were dying at the same rate.

Mr. Coughlin was coming closer to us. I could hear his heavy breathing and the frozen grass crunching beneath every step he took. He decided that he wanted to put the final nail in the coffin, so he kicked our hands away from each other and stood between us. He then pointed his gun at Sadie.

Three shots let out ... but they weren't from his gun.

The gunshots that rang out pierced into Mr. Coughlin's back and through his chest before he could pull the trigger. Mrs. Coughlin had finally come to Sadie's aid.

But she was too late.

If she had ran into the house to grab her husband's other gun a few minutes earlier, our bodies wouldn't have been sunken into the muddy grass, and Sadie's eyes would have been full of life.

Instead, death was knocking at our doors, and it turned its attention to my darling. I could see in her eyes that she was leaving. I didn't want to live without her. I didn't want her to leave me, so I pleaded with her, but my words sounded like air being pushed through a straw.

I wish she heard me ...

CHAPTER SIX

"What did you plead, Nicholi?"

"I ..."

"What did you ask? Don't drift away. *Tell me.*"

"It's pointless. She didn't hear me."

I woke up to the sound of the EKG, with an IV in my arm and the whispering of my parents beside me. I opened my eyes slowly, feeling dizzy and unsteady, and for a moment I didn't realize where I was. I thought it was all a dream until reality hit, and it hit hard. The doctors, nurses, and everyone in the general area had to restrain me back into bed. I remember screaming out for Sadie and then everything went black again. I was put back into a deep sleep, and I wouldn't wake for several hours.

When I woke up, I was heavily drugged and slow thinking, but whatever they had given me had only calmed my body, not my soul; I was still in deep, deep darkness.

"Nicky?" my mother spoke softly. I could hear the concern in her voice as she clicked the nurse-call button.

A nurse came into the room immediately. "Hello, Nicholi. We're really glad to see those eyes of yours. You're a fighter."

I could barely speak—my throat was as dry as a clay pot on a sunny day—but I'd be damned if I didn't ask. I was afraid to hear the truth, but I needed to know.

"Where's Sadie?" I let out, although I somehow already knew. But there was still that small hope—that one miracle I believed GOD had owed me that I never cashed in.

The nurse looked grim and asked if my parents would like to tell me.

"Sadie didn't make it, son," my father confirmed, as he placed his hand on my shoulder and my mother placed her hand in mine. Even though I had already known it in my heart, the confirmation felt as if she had died all over again. The truth was now cemented, and hope was gone forever.

I shrugged my parents off of me. Their touch felt wrong. I didn't want the people who could have stopped this from happening years ago to touch me. It made me sick to my stomach.

I closed my eyes and tried to think of anything else out of hope of distracting my mind because I felt like I was slipping away; I felt my sanity abandoning me. I fought for control by trying to remember better times, and my thoughts took me to a time when Sadie was a little girl—the little girl who had claimed my heart from the start. I wanted to stay in those memories where we innocently enjoyed each other's company, where I could hear her laugh before her cries ever began, where I could see the joy in her eyes before the pain came. It was all too much, but I was beyond the point of crying. I was in shock. I couldn't believe that I was forced to live a life without her. All I ever known was her—she *was* my life. When I opened my eyes, no emotion was upon my face, and I remained silent as I stared at the small cracks and bumps on the hospital wall in front of me. I felt nothingness. I felt void. I felt robotic. I felt soulless. Sadie was the source of my life, and when she went, *so did I.*

I was released from the hospital two weeks later. My parents were by my side assisting my every move as I walked with a cane to the car. I hated that I needed their help.

When my parents pulled into the driveway of our home (this home), I threw open the car door and made my way out. I couldn't take it anymore. I needed to know.

"Where are you going?" my mother asked.

I ignored her and kept walking. But walking was a struggle, and I ultimately fell to the ground.

My parents rushed over and picked me up.

"Where are you going, Nicky?" my mother asked again.

"I need to know," I said, as I looked into the distance at Sadie's childhood home.

Mom and dad looked at each other in utter confusion.

I, again, attempted to walk, and they assisted me.

Once we were out of the tall grass, I stopped. "You can leave me here," I told them. "I need to do this alone."

They accepted it and stood back.

I pounded on every door and even on the side paneling of that house, the same way Sadie did when she was calling out to Mr. Coughlin. I, like her, had reached a state of madness.

The side door eventually opened, and it opened as if it carried the heavy burden of that home. Standing in the doorway, was Mrs. Coughlin. She was no longer vibrant and filled with life the way Sadie and I had seen her. She had returned to her past—gloom made its home in her and seeped through her pores. Although she was no longer tortured by Mr. Coughlin, she was now tortured by her own choices, tortured by the screaming inside of her soul that wished she could turn back the hands time.

"Who's Jimmy!" I shouted at her before she could even get a breath out.

She looked to her side, closed her eyes, and welcomed me in.

I walked in and wasted no time asking her again.

She remained silent and walked over to the cabinet in the kitchen, where she took out two pills and swallowed them with a glass of water.

I continued to bombard her. "Your husband ... I keep hearing him screaming out this name. It haunts me in my dreams and every waking day of my life. *Who is Jimmy?*"

For a moment, it seemed like she was going to speak, but then she shook her head and walked past me.

I was relentless. I stood in front of her and demanded an answer. "I lost the love my life, *my best friend*. Answer me!"

She lifted her head up and looked directly in my eyes, and said, "I lost two of mine." She then dropped her head and took a deep breath. "I had to kill my husband because of my mistake. And my child, *my precious child*, died because of it."

My mind betrayed me then. It had flooded me with images of Sadie dying, and I had to fight away the rage that came with them because I needed to listen to her. I knew in my gut that she held the answer.

"Jimmy ..." she continued. "Jimmy was Anthony's best friend. They grew up together, served in the same war and in the same unit. They'd always say that they were closer than blood brothers. What was Anthony's was Jimmy's and what was Jimmy's was Anthony's, except for me."

My leg began to ache from standing on it for too long, so I leaned on the corner of the table and listened to Mrs. Coughlin's tale of regret.

"Jimmy came home from the war earlier than Anthony, and he made a promise to him that he would look after me. He kept that promise. He mowed the lawn, brought me to and from the grocery store, fixed my car whenever the damn thing decided not to run. He was wonderful. It wasn't his fault—*it was mine.* I became lonely and needy and started calling him to come over for every little thing just because I wanted someone to talk to. I needed someone to fill the void that Anthony left."

"What are you saying?"

"I tried to tell her, Nicholi, but I couldn't get the words out."

"What are you saying?"

"It was only one night, and I felt regret immediately after. I just … I needed a man's touch. It had been so long since I had been held."

My heart began to race, and I could hear Mr. Coughlin crying out in my head: *You were my friend, Jimmy! You were my best friend. Why'd you do it!*

"It's my fault," she continued. "I gave him too much wine, and I seduced him. He told me we shouldn't, but I kept throwing myself at him until he gave in."

I couldn't believe my ears.

"A week later, I got a call from the army telling me that Anthony had been hurt and was being medically discharged. A week after that he was home and then eight months and two weeks later, Sadie came into this world. Jimmy and I had an agreement: he promised that he wouldn't speak of that night. But when he saw Sadie in the hospital, he fell in love with her. It was impossible for him to keep our secret after that.

"It was a few days before Sadie's first birthday when Jimmy decided to break his silence—and then Anthony broke his jaw. If he were anyone else, Anthony would have killed him right then and there. But Jimmy was a brother to him, so he warned him to never show his face again. And he didn't.

"The years following, I thought we would make it as a family. I thought the past had finally let go of its grip on us. I thought we had found a silver lining. Anthony had learned to love and adore Sadie when she was a toddler. But around 10 years old, Sadie became a constant reminder that she wasn't his through the undeniable mannerisms she shared with Jimmy and a beauty mark that was uniquely like the one he had on his head. I watched Anthony struggle with it every day. Every time he was reminded that Sadie wasn't his, he was also reminded that he once lost me.

"It was all too much for Anthony to take. He couldn't pretend to not see what was clearly in front of him every day, so he tried to stay away, and he found comfort at the bar with its plethora of numbing drinks. He'd come home late in the middle of the night, stumbling and slurring, and it was fine at first. I understood. But everything changed one night when Sadie innocently came out of her room to see if he was okay. 'Papa, are you okay?' she asked."

As Mrs. Coughlin spoke, I could hear Sadie calling out desperately to the man who she thought was her father: *Papa! Open the door! It's me!*

Mrs. Coughlin continued, "He hit her for the first time that night, and when I tried to step in, he hit me, too. It was never the same after that. He had found false justice. He found a relief that the alcohol no longer provided. In a demonic way, he was fighting back."

"*Enough*," I said. I couldn't bear hearing anymore. She had given me the answer to the question that ate at me. There was no more I needed to know, so I stood up straight and began to make my way out.

"It's my fault, it's my fault ... it's my fault," Mrs. Coughlin repeatedly whispered to herself, as if torturing herself by saying it over and over again would bring justice.

As I stood in the doorway with my back to her, I had a choice to make. I could console her or I could leave.

I left.

I left that house and never went back. I left Sadie's mother—the one Sadie loved unconditionally—alone to torture herself. It's one of my biggest regrets. I should've been a better man. That was the one time I didn't think about Sadie because I only thought about myself. I thought about my own justice.

In my eyes, Mrs. Coughlin was never Sadie's mother, Daji was. And it was time for me to go back home and tell her that her daughter was gone ... forever.

I didn't go back that day, though. In fact, it took me four months to work up the courage. I didn't know how to tell her. At one point, I thought it might be best for her to think that we had left and never returned, but I couldn't do that to her. I would have rather her fall to pieces *with* me than to crumble because of me. She needed to know the truth, and she needed *me*.

* * * *

It was a fall day when I arrived back in town. Leaves fell to the ground, trees wept—death was all around me. And here I was bringing its message to a woman so full of life.

I walked up the steps and stood in front Daji's door as if I were a stranger. I was sick to my stomach. I felt like I didn't deserve her after I had left her alone for so long. I should've told her sooner. I should've been there for her, but it was my guilt that kept me away. I felt like I contributed to Sadie's death because I should've demanded that she not go back. I held the key to our destiny, and I threw it all away out of fear of hurting her feelings.

I took a deep breath, raised my trembling hand and knocked on the door.

It opened slowly. Daji looked like she had been crying without rest, and when she realized that it was me, and that I was alone, she frantically shook her head in denial and cried out. Someone had already told her.

Behind her were boxes filled with our belongings from our apartment. The landlord had called her since she was our co-signer because he hadn't received his rent. After threatening to throw our stuff out, she paid to have it delivered to her. She tried to reach out to us through every means possible, and when she didn't hear from us, she contacted our college. That's when she got the news.

She took the red-eye out to the hospital in search for me, but when she arrived, I had already been released two months prior. And the hospital couldn't, by policy, tell her with whom I left and where I went. She called everywhere in hope for some information on us, like where Sadie was laid to rest and where I could've been, but she was given no answers.

She cried day and night. Her mind raced with thoughts of Sadie rotting away in the ground and me wandering the world wounded and alone. She placed a heavy burden on herself for not being there to help us even though there was nothing she could've done, but that's what mothers do.

And here I was, standing at her doorstep—wounded and alone. I stood in silence as she wailed. No words I could've said would have calmed her. She was *completely* without peace. She was devastated. She was broken beyond repair. I wanted to hold her, but I didn't feel worthy. She had spent all this time in misery alone because I was too afraid to face her. I should have gone to her as soon as I could, but I waited. I was coward.

"I'm so sorry," I exhaled, my words barely making it out of my mouth. "You shouldn't have found out this way. I should've been here …" I didn't know what else to say, so I turned around to exile myself. I made my way down the steps, but then Daji screamed from the depths of her agony, "Nicholi!"

I stood with my back to her, my eyes unable to hold their waters. I couldn't turn around. I didn't want her to see me like that.

Her voice trembled. "Don't g-go. *Please*, d-don't g-go."

I listened to my mother. I turned around and walked back to her with my head to the ground in shame, and she grabbed me tight and wept on my chest.

"I don't think that I can stay," I told her as I looked at our boxes on the floor behind her and then around the home that Sadie loved so dearly. Everywhere that I placed my eyes I was tortured with memories. I looked in the kitchen and saw Sadie and Daji baking and dancing together. I looked in the living room and saw Sadie cracking up as she and Daji fought over the blanket while watching a movie. I looked toward the stairs and saw the time they laughed hysterically as they refolded all of the clean clothes because Sadie had tripped on the way up. I looked toward the basement door and remembered the day Sadie and I fell in love ...

Daji had been in the basement all day and wouldn't let us see what she was up to. When the afternoon came around, music began to play in the basement. At the time, I was on the couch in the living room watching TV, and Sadie was across from me on the loveseat reading a book. We looked at each other wondering what in the world Daji could've been doing down there all day. The music being played was the commercial hits that you would hear on the radio—the music of our age—and Sadie seemed to enjoy it because she began to bob her head.

"You like this?" I said.

"Stop ... Don't make fun of me, Nicky!"

I teased her and laughed.

"It's catchy. Don't judge me!" she said, pointing a warning finger at me.

"Nicholi! Sadie!" Daji called for us.

We jumped up, excited to see what the big mystery was, and ran downstairs.

To our surprise, Daji had decorated the entire basement. There was a punch bowl sitting on a table, drapes and banners with her school's colors and mascot, a rotating disco ball hanging from the ceiling, and a "DJ" booth that was basically a folding table with a laptop on top of it.

Sadie chuckled. "What is all of this?"

"As you two know, tomorrow is my school's prom. And, well, I felt bad that you two couldn't experience it. Every teenager deserves this experience. And since you can't come with me, I wanted to give you one."

"Aww!" Sadie exclaimed.

I was speechless.

Daji walked to the closet, which was now hidden behind a curtain, and pulled out a suit and a dress. With both in her hands, she came to me first. "You, sir, are going to get dressed like the gentleman that you are."

"I have to wear this?"

"Yes, you do. And you're going to do what every young man does for his date ... wait."

My eyebrows crinkled.

She then took Sadie by the hand.

"Hold on. How long do I have to wait for?"

Daji patted me on the shoulder. "For as long as it takes a girl to get ready."

Sadie perked up with a smile from ear to ear, and they skipped up the stairs like two best friends ready to gossip.

I got ready in ten minutes, and had to wait another fifty for Sadie.

I was in the kitchen eating some apple pie when Daji came in. She placed her hand on her hips and shook her head.

"Nicholi …"

"What?" I asked, with my mouth full of pie.

She gestured for me to come to her, and I did.

"You call this getting ready?"

"What? I put on the suit."

She shook her head again and grabbed me by the collar. She then brought me to the bathroom, gelled my hair, fixed my tie and handed me a toothbrush. "Boy, no girl wants to smell your pie breath when you dance with her."

I laughed and took the toothbrush from her. When I finished brushing my teeth, she grabbed my hand and escorted me downstairs.

"Where's Sadie?" I asked.

Daji grinned. "You have a lot to learn, Nicholi. A girl never shows up on time. Wait here."

"I have to wait again?"

Daji skipped upstairs.

Five minutes later, I heard the door open and both of their footsteps making their way down the stairs.

"Wait!" Daji told Sadie. She then ran down the stairs ahead of her, stood beside me and held up her camera. "Okay, now!"

Sadie walked gently down the stairs in her heels and burgundy laced dress; her curls bounced with every step she took. Never had my eyes been more fixated on anyone or anything. She took my breath away, and she seemed to have the same reaction when she saw me. We never looked at each other as we had in that moment.

Daji nudged me. "Don't you have something to say?"

I was speechless.

Daji walked up to Sadie and looked over at me, widening her eyes and raising her brows. "Doesn't she look great?" she said, between her teeth.

I gulped. "Um … wow." I had to catch my breath. "You—"

"You look very handsome, Nicky," Sadie said.

"You're the most beautiful thing I've ever seen," I blurted out. I quickly realized what I had said and stumbled over my words to clarify. "Not 'thing' … I mean … um …"

Sadie grinned. "Thank you, Nicky."

"DJ's in the house!" Daji shouted out, breaking the pheromone-induced passion between us. She put on her oversized headphones and waved her hands in the air as she walked over to the DJ table. Sadie and I laughed so hard that tears nearly fell from our eyes. Daji was always childlike, so full of life and joy.

"Oh, my pies!" Daji exclaimed, hearing her portable kitchen timer ring. She ran upstairs to take them out, leaving Sadie and I alone.

The song Sadie was bobbing her head to earlier came back on, and she immediately pointed her finger at me. "Don't judge me."

She was expecting me to tease her, but I was over that. I just wanted to dance with her—and I hated dancing.

"Would you ... like to dance?" I nervously asked, as if I hadn't known her my whole life.

She smiled and placed her hands on my shoulders.

There was that passion again. I've held her many times, but never like this.

"Nicky ..." Sadie said.

"Yes?"

"Um ..."

I already knew what my darling wanted. Her eyes were always able to speak to me in ways her tongue could not. I kissed her. And nothing had ever felt more right in my life.

"Children!" Daji shouted from upstairs. "Dessert is ready!"

Sadie stepped back and nervously straightened her dress. "I guess we should, um ..."

I took a deep breath and nodded.

We walked upstairs and Daji, with a pie in her hand, raised her brow and sucked her teeth.

Did she know that we kissed? Sadie and I asked each other with our eyes.

"Come here, Nicky," Daji said, putting down the pie and walking toward me. "You should know that a king always glows when he kisses his queen."

Sadie and I turned red. How did she know?

"You should also know"—she turned to Sadie—"that lipstick does not discriminate between lips when they meet." Daji pulled out a napkin from her apron and wiped my mouth.

Sadie and I had been caught red-handed. We couldn't help but laugh, and Daji smirked.

"Now come. Help me bring these pies downstairs. Let's get this party started!" Daji shouted with glee.

I kept looking at that basement door, trying to cling on to that memory as long as I could.

"Please d-don't g-go, Nicky," Daji continued to weep.

She was there when Sadie and I needed her, and now she needed me. It was my turn to be there for her, so I held her and walked back into our home.

I'd like to tell you that our lives were fine after that, that we learned to pick up the pieces and moved on, but the fact is that our home was never the same.

Daji was never the same.

She walked around the house most days just because she *had* to. She was alive, but not living. There was no more joy in her. She did, however, try to fake her happiness for me, but the sorrow in her eyes told her truth. And one day, eight months after I knocked on her door, all of the pain that had built up in her heart had finally run out of room.

It was the evening of Sadie's birthday. Daji wanted to celebrate in memory of her. We were cooking dinner and the music was playing softly in the background when a plate suddenly fell out of her hand. I stopped cutting the onions and looked up quickly, and to my horror, I saw her grabbing her chest. Almost instantly, her knees gave out and I reached out to grab her, but there was nothing I could do. All I could do was hold her.

She gasped for air and clung to my shirt, but then peace washed over her. I know this because her eyes opened wide in awe, and she *smiled*.

Daji passed away from severe heartache. But in the end, I'd like to think it was restored. I'd like to think that she smiled because Sadie was waiting for her.

CHAPTER SEVEN

"When will the sun rise? It should have risen by now, no?"

"Maybe the new day waits for you to finish your story. Maybe it can't move forward until you do. Continue, Nicholi. I have faith the light will come soon enough."

I was now without love, devoid entirely of happiness. I got a call from Daji's lawyer, asking me to go in to discuss arrangements for her.

"Nicholi, it's nice to meet you. Tristan Baker," he said, stretching out his hand. "My condolences."

I nodded, not knowing what to say, and shook his hand.

"Please, take a seat."

I sat and listened to him.

"I asked you to come in to discuss important matters

regarding Diana's will. She states that everything should be left to you. However, she left very little instruction as to what to do for her funeral arrangements."

I didn't know what to say. I didn't have the slightest idea of how to plan a funeral, so I spoke to him honestly. "Sir, I need someone to guide me through this. I've never even been to a funeral. I don't know what to do, nor can I afford one. Is there a way I can take out a loan? You said she left everything in my name, so can I sell the house to pay for it?"

"That *would* be a way of obtaining income, but not enough time. Her body must be buried by the week's end."

Again, I didn't know what to say. I had no money.

But then he came up with an idea. "Diana's paperwork shows that she has a sibling, a sister."

"Biologically? Yes. I was told she had a half-sister, but she's no sister of hers," I said crudely.

"Well, Diana left this letter." He went into his drawer and placed it in front of me on the table. It was ivory white and on the front of it she wrote: *To my beloved sister.* "Diana asked, in her will, for you to read it to her sister. Perhaps—and this is up to you—we can reach out to her and see if she's willing to handle the financial end of Diana's funeral."

"She has no family except for me," I responded without even taking a breath.

"I understand," he said. "But we either make the call or she gets laid to rest with the unclaimed bodies of the state. Is that where you want her to be?"

My head dropped.

"What if I spoke to them on your behalf?" he asked.

Everything in me said to refuse, but then I thought about all that she had given Sadie and I. She deserved a proper burial. "*Fine*. Make the call."

He continued to be as transparent as possible with me. "You do know that they may want to attend the service. Will you be okay with that?"

I was sick to my stomach. Do I refuse and allow Daji to be laid to rest among the lost or do I allow the very person that made her feel lost attend the ceremony where she should be at rest? What rest would that be?

Again, I put aside my pride. "Make the call."

He was relieved to hear me agree and gave me paperwork to sign. The paperwork was for the possession of everything that was hers: from her home to the garments in it, everything was mine. But I would have given it all away just to be with her one more day.

* * * *

The day of the funeral came. Daji's sister, thankfully, agreed to cover all expenses. It was a rainy, dark day—which made me sick to think that even on her day of rest a black cloud was over her.

I sat in the car and watched from a distance as two people stood beside the casket with their heads down, one consoling the other. I was too far to see their faces, and I didn't want to join them until the pastor (Maryanne) showed up because I didn't want to witness their crocodile tears for longer than I had to. When she finally arrived, I stepped out of the car and walked toward the burial service with my head to the ground. I remember staring at the mud that was rising through the grass and surrounding my shoes with every step that I took. I tried to focus on anything other than the anger that was burning inside of me. But then, that anger became rage when I heard my name called out by an unmistakable voice.

"Nicky? Nicky, what are you doing here?"

I looked up and saw my mother with my father beside her.

"What are you doing here?" she asked again.

I couldn't believe my eyes.

"It was you?" I stepped back, shaking my head. "This ... this can't be."

"Why are you here, honey?"

"You're ... you're her sister?"

I paced back and forth next to the casket, unable to understand the reality of the situation.

"Yes. This is my baby sister. We were estranged. Who

told you to come here?"

Breathing heavily, I pointed at the casket. "Do you know why she died?"

My mother's face was blank.

"Do you know why she died!" I shouted.

My mother's eyes looked into the distance. "They said it was due to a heart atta—"

"Wrong!" I screamed. My mother stepped back as I walked directly in front of her, my eyes piercing into hers. "She died of heartache! She died because of you! You left her alone—just like you left Sadie. They both died because of *you!*"

My father tried to get a word in. "Nich—"

"All she wanted was a family," I continued.

"I didn't do anything!" my mother shouted back. That was the first time I had ever heard her raise her voice. The guilt she felt was surfacing.

"That's exactly it. You did *nothing.*" I pointed at the casket again. "*You* should be the one in here, not her!"

My mother gasped and misery fell upon her as heavy as the day's rain.

I was enraged, but that rage quickly turned into deep sorrow as I walked over to the casket. I fell to my knees, kissed it, and told Daji that I loved her. I promised her that she'd always be remembered and never lost, that unlike her sister, I'd keep her. I then got up, turned to Maryanne, apologized to her, and asked her to continue without me.

But then, I remembered the letter.

"Forgive me," I said, interrupting Maryanne's prayer.

She nodded and closed her Bible.

With trembling hands, I took out the letter from my pocket and read it out loud—for the first time—as Daji wished. It was one of the hardest things I've ever had to do. I could hear her voice in my head through her words.

My dear sister,

You left me when I needed you most, but on this day I leave you. And although you left me with nothing, I leave you with love. I have been lonely most of my life because of you, but the one who is reading this letter has given me a new life. He, along with the one I join today, showed me the love that I longed for. And that love has overflowed my heart so much that I now give it to you. I forgive you, I really do. Please tell my nephew that although he has never met me, I love—"

I couldn't finish the letter. She was expressing her love for me and didn't even know that she had already given me much more. I threw the letter on the ground next to my mother's feet and walked away.

I never saw my parents again after that. I deserted them the same way they deserted Daji and Sadie.

CHAPTER EIGHT

"Where do you think Daji and Sadie are now?"

"I don't know, but if heaven was to exist, I'm sure the angels welcomed them with open arms and the good LORD presented himself to them."

"What do you think heaven is like?"

"I wouldn't be the best person to answer that question."

"I think it's like a marketplace, a place where everyone is always together, joyful and fruitful in every sense of the word, and everyone is content in knowing that all they will ever need is theirs for the taking—a marketplace that gives endlessly and people take eternally. Wouldn't you like to go to a place like this, Nicholi?"

"I want to go where Sadie is."

"What do you think hell is like?"

"*Hell is life.*"

"That can't be true."

"Why not?"

"Because where there is hope, hell cannot be. The living have hope, no matter how small and insignificant it may seem."

"I didn't always have hope in my life. In fact, I once lost it entirely. It is my greatest regret, and it still haunts me today. It gives reason to my deserved misery."

"What did you do?"

The years flew past me, and I was now a depressed 35-year-old drunk, who was a helper for a construction company with no future ambitions, sitting at a bar demanding more drinks.

"I think you've had enough, don't you?" the bartender said.

I grumbled beneath my breath, my eyes beet red and my head barely lifting up from the counter; I treated the bar top as if it was my own personal pillow.

"Excuse me?" she egged on.

"What!" I snapped.

"I think you had enough. You should leave."

"Enough?" I laughed at her suggestion and, once again, grumbled beneath my breath.

She continued to carry on the fight. "Excuse me?"

She had now exasperated my patience. "Am I a child?

Are you my babysitter? Who sent you to watch over me?"

She stared at my drink with pure hatred.

"What? You don't like that I'm drinking? News flash, young lady, you work at a *bar*. When I say I've had enough, then I've had enough. But not you or anyone else will decide that."

"You're going to ruin your life if you keep drinking like this."

"Life?" I cynically chuckled. "Tell me what you know about life."

She remained quiet.

"That's right, *nothing*. You don't know a damn thing. I bet you have big dreams and goals, right? Well let me break this to you. Don't count on anything you can't see in front of you, and don't count a minute ahead of the present. And then maybe—and that's a *slim* maybe—you'll make it through life." I began to laugh as if I heard a classic joke. "Ha! *Life* she says! You naïve young girl, you have *false* hope. There's much more lows than highs in the thing you call life. The only highs that will come in your life are those tits on your chest, and even they will soon follow the laws of this 'life' that you speak of. They, too, will drop to their sorry reality."

"*Stop it*. You don't mean that." I saw her innocent eyes tear up, yet I continued to antagonize.

"I don't? I'm pretty sure that I do."

"You're going to be an old, sad man if you keep drinking like this," she pushed on.

I scowled at her as if she was the cause of my pain, placing blame on her for my misery when all she tried to do was help me. "*So be it!* The sadness has already come for me, and I sleep in its darkness. My pillow rests on its headboard and my body is swallowed by its comfort. The only thing missing is the old age—and it's creeping up, honey! Oh, sweet death, come and take me before my time!" I yelled at the top of my lungs, and suddenly the bar grew quiet. The music that was playing in the background turned off, and everyone stared at me with concerned eyes.

"What are all of you looking at? She started it!" I pointed in her direction, like a child drawing attention away from himself. Everyone continued to stare as if I had lost my mind.

"Where'd she go? She was just here ..." I scratched my head. "She was ... she was *here*," I said once more, thinking of Sadie.

Embarrassed, I got up to leave as quickly as I could, which wasn't quick at all. An 80-year-old man with one leg could've done it in faster time.

When I got home, I kept hearing her voice in my head: *You're going to end up an old, sad man.*

I lied in bed and was tortured by the horrific things I said to her: *The sadness has already come for me, and I sleep in its darkness. My pillow rests on its headboard and my body is swallowed by its comfort.*

I couldn't rest, so I got up and opened the fridge to grab a beer. I was going to do what I did best—drink away my problems. But I was still haunted by my words: *Oh, sweet death, come and take me before my time!* Those words ran through my mind over and over and over again. It was driving me mad. I tried to shake it, but there was no hope. I was guilty of unleashing demonic words onto a sweet girl whose only wish was for me to stop killing myself.

I was nearly pulling my hair out from the torment, so I walked into my bathroom to splash cold water on my face in hope that it would force my mind to focus on anything other than my words. It seemed to have worked at first, but as I patted my face with a towel, I was forced to face the monster I had become. I saw a man in the mirror that I could no longer recognize as myself. I was only 35, yet I had bags under my eyes that resembled a man twice my age, a beard that grew low and close to my Adam's apple that was peppered with white hair, and skin as red as a pale man on a sunny day.

And although I could not recognize myself, this man in the mirror was all too familiar. He resembled *someone*. I stared into that mirror, looking into my own eyes, trying to decipher who it was that I was looking at. I soon realized that my actions, my words and *now* my appearance resembled the person I despised most. Mr. Coughlin had taken away the love of my life, which then contributed to the loss of my aunt, who became my mother, and now he had taken mine: my hate for him consumed me so much that I became him.

I couldn't let that continue.

I was determined to do what I thought I should have done from the beginning. I wasn't going to let him live, *not through me*.

I shouted like a psychotic man at the mirror as if I was speaking directly to him, circling back and forth and nearly tearing the skin off of my face. I clawed at myself, spat and smashed every mirror in my home except for one. I left the mirror in the living room just above my desk untouched. I wanted to watch Mr. Coughlin's life fade away.

Adrenaline ran through me like never before. There was no calming me. I moved my couch from underneath the ceiling fan and placed it against the entrance door so that no one could enter. I then went into my toolbox and took out a 1-inch, heavy braided nylon rope. But when I took it out, fear consumed me. It consumed me so much that I ran back to the bathroom and threw up on top of the shattered glass in the sink. In that moment, I questioned my plan. But all I had to do was go back into the living room and look into that mirror again. The wicked resemblance between me and Mr. Coughlin allowed my fear to be replaced with despair and rage.

I took out my one-foot stool, stood on it, secured the rope to the ceiling fan and then tied a bowknot. It was the only type of knot I could think of to use. I figured if they used it on horses, it would work on me. I then put my neck through the loop and tied my hands in front of me.

There I was looking into the mirror, fantasizing that I was staring him down. "It's over," I said. "It's *finally* over. *You lose.*"

With those words, I pushed off the stool with my toes. My neck didn't snap as I had planned. Instead, I was slowly suffocating. I felt the rope tearing through the skin of my neck as the weight of my body pulled down on it. If I told you that I continued to stare down the illusion of Mr. Coughlin in the mirror, I'd be a liar. I was scared shitless. My lungs, instinctively, fought a losing battle to take in air. My nerves desperately jerked my body to free itself. The veins in my neck felt like boiling water was rushing through them as my blood had become trapped in its path. My pants were soaked from my own piss. My ears popped, and my eyes felt like they were going to burst out of their sockets. And then, finally, I exhaled and everything faded to black.

Just as I had hoped, there she was—my sweet Sadie, my darling. Yards away, as far as my childhood home was to hers, Sadie stood in the distance. It's as if we were floating in a space devoid of stars and planets—surrounded by nothingness. Yet in this void of space and time, I had everything.

A beaming, constant light shined from above directly on her. She looked up and then at me. It's as if the light was calling her, but every time she chose to look in my direction, that light became dimmer and dimmer.

She stood silently looking up and then at me for a while until she finally made her decision. She stepped away and entered into the void. She chose me. She chose me over heaven. She was a fool. She was a fool for love. She was a fool to think that I was her heaven, even though I knew she was mine. We were two foolish lovers, soul mates who refused to be separated even in death. But the farther she got from the light, the more somber her gaze became.

It took everything in me to walk toward her. My soul was weak. It felt like the weight of the world was on me, but the reality was that it was much more than that—both of our worlds weighed on me.

When I was finally in arm's length from her, I saw horror in her eyes. She shook her head uncontrollably and placed her hand over her lips as she stared at me.

I reached out to touch her, but she moved away.

"No!" she screamed, although I could not hear her; I could only read her lips. All that I was allowed to hear was my own heartbeat. And as the time passed, it slowed.

I tried to step closer to her, but I could not move any farther. There was an invisible force that held me back, and the more that I tried, the more tired I became.

Again, although I could not hear her, I could see her desperately pleading to me. She was in a deeper anguish than I had ever seen—more pain than Mr. Coughlin had ever caused—*and I was the reason*. I had placed myself in this void ... and forced her in it.

"Sa—" I couldn't finish my sentence. My throat was restrained by another force that was now pulling me back by my neck. It felt like I was being sucked into a vacuum. I extended my hands like a child being dragged away, and she was hysterical.

The void had now turned into the room that I was hanging in, and I witnessed Sadie crying at my feet, shaking uncontrollably. I walked over to her—this time without anything holding me back—and kneeled down to show her that I was okay, that I was right beside her.

She didn't respond.

I was placed back in the room that I had given up hope only to find myself *helpless*. I no longer had a choice. I had taken that away from myself. And my darling, because she loved me so much, would spend an eternity crying for me, and I would spend it tortured by the sight.

"I love you, Sadie," I said, not expecting a response. But then she turned to me and said, "If you love me, you will live."

I stepped back in shock.

She repeated herself. "If you love me … *you will live!*" She then got up from her knees and shook my body that was hanging. "Live!" she screamed.

In this moment, I, once again, felt the rope tearing through the skin of my neck as the weight of my body pulled down on it. It's as if my mind and soul kept slipping in and out of the realities of life and death: in life, my body jerked uncontrollably; in death, Sadie shook it.

"Live!" she continued to scream.

I would've gladly stood in a room with my Sadie for eternity, but not like this. I couldn't bear this torment—I couldn't bear being the reason for my darling's eternal despair. So I agreed to live, and as soon as I did, the fan ripped from the ceiling and I fell to the ground with it.

Since the bowknot was made for tension and tension was no longer applied, it loosened just enough for me to gasp for air. I passed out within seconds after falling to the ground. I didn't dream. I didn't see anything. In fact, it felt like I had only closed my eyes for a few seconds, but I knew many hours had passed because the sun was rising when I reopened them. I awoke in great pain, but it was nothing compared to the agony I felt witnessing Sadie in misery because of my own doing. Like you said, I had hope. And hope, no matter how small and insignificant it may have seemed, was enough to get me up. It took some time, but I eventually found the strength to get myself to the emergency room.

CHAPTER NINE

"What was life like after that fear of damnation? What did you do with your second chance?"

"I reset my life."

"How?"

"I started with a pair of clippers."

When I got out of the hospital, the first thing I did was go back home and look back into that mirror, back into the eyes of the man I hated, back into the eyes of the man that I had despised so much that I *almost* became.

I took out my clippers from my drawer, plugged it into the wall, shaved … and wept. I didn't stop at my beard, either; I shaved my head, too. After that, I threw out every alcoholic beverage and cleaned my apartment, top to bottom. I knew that in order to get through the pain of my past, I had to face it for once without an escape. I had spent so many years of my life running away. The success of running away with Sadie gave me reason to continue that pattern into my adult life. And when I couldn't physically get up and go, I escaped my reality by binge drinking. I ran away from my problems every way possible until I inevitably ran out of ways to run, and then I tried to escape entirely by ending my life. But I had made a mistake in believing that I could kill Mr. Coughlin by harming myself. It wasn't until the fear of self-conflicted death that I realized that the only way to truly overcome my demons, or demon, is to *live* my life.

But that was easier said than done because without the escape of alcohol my mind never rested, and the lack of endorphins in my sober brain had caused havoc on my mental state. I constantly had racing thoughts, especially at night, and so insomnia became my new soul mate. And if I dared to cheat on her with two or three hours of sleep, I'd wake up screaming in cold sweats.

It felt like I had escaped one hell only to live in another, but the irony of it all was that a blessing actually came out of that insomnia—out of what I sworn was a curse—because if it weren't for those sleepless nights, I wouldn't have found rest in Mila.

Since I could not sleep and was a perpetual victim to the silence of the night and the loneliness that came with it, I found company in the flickering light that pierced through the shades of my window from the diner's broken sign across the street.

One early morning, around four, I decided to walk into that diner. That was one of the best decisions of my life because there she was, with her red hair wrapped tightly in a bun and a smile that could shed light on the darkest places. No one could have ever known the struggle she was going through. No one could've known she was a widow living paycheck to paycheck to support her daughter. No one could've seen behind the concealer that hid the dark circles around her eyes. I, like many, sat at the counter that morning and was drawn to her beauty.

"Good morning," Mila said, with a smile she gave every customer. I was mesmerized by her red lipstick, her perfect teeth, and the three freckles above her nose. I laugh now thinking about it because of my ignorance back then: I thought I was special.

"*Good morning*," she said again, this time with a giggle. Her giggle reminded me of Sadie's, so right there and then my bliss of being in awe of her beauty was crushed.

"Never mind," I said, quickly getting up to leave. I was ashamed of myself for even thinking about another woman.

"Well, that was rude," she said jokingly, but it reminded me of that day when I argued with the young bartender. I needed to redeem myself, so I turned back around.

"Changed your mind?" she asked, smirking.

"You're good. Is this how you get everyone to stay here, by guilt-tripping them?"

"Maybe," she answered, turning her back. "What can I get for you? You look like you need a good cup of Joe."

"You can give me a cup of Jimmy, a cup of George— *whatever you want to call it*—as long as there is coffee in that cup."

There was that giggle again.

I put my head down, closed my eyes and spoke to Sadie: *You're not forgotten.*

Mila placed a cup in front of me. "How about a cup of tea instead? It's healthier and does the same job. We can call it a cup of Julie."

I laughed, for once. I hadn't laughed in a long time. It felt foreign to me. It was all too much too soon. It didn't feel right, so I told her that I'd take it to go.

She gave me a friendly nod, and I walked out the door and back into my apartment. I placed my chair by the window, pulled up the shade, and watched the light from the diner's sign flicker as I watched the sun come up with my tea in hand.

I didn't go back to that diner the next day or the day after. Instead, I stood up during those nights—as I had become accustom to—and continued to stare at that sign. I couldn't get myself to move on from Sadie; she was all I've ever known.

It took me a month from that day to return to the diner. And when I did, Mila welcomed me with that smile of hers.

"Welcome back. Can I get you another cup of Julie?"

She remembered me. I felt special again.

"Yes. A cup of Julie would be great." With those words, I accepted the possibility of a future. Whether we'd just be friends or she'd become the next love of my life, I didn't know—but I accepted it all.

I didn't say much to her that day or any other day for the next few weeks, but I did go into that diner like clockwork every morning at 5:30. I became a regular and Mila noticed. She was great at conversing, something I was not particularly skilled at since I had no experience talking to women. I was always thinking of smooth things to say, yet I could never articulate my thoughts. I constantly stumbled over my words, but she made me feel comfortable. She made me laugh. She filled my heart for 30 minutes every day. I eventually overcame my shyness and began to converse with her fluently. From then on, my presence at the diner was just as important to her as hers was to me.

Through our friendship, she opened up and told me about her life and her late husband that passed away from a car crash. She was pregnant at the time with no insurance and overwhelmed with bills that she could never pay off. So with no college degree and a child on the way, she was forced to work nights into the early mornings at the diner. And she did this for years.

Every time she'd tell me about her life, she'd cover up her pain with the same joke: "We're two miserable people, aren't we?"

Usually I'd nod in agreement, but on one particular day I realized that that was no longer true, so I shook my head and said something I never thought I would: "Not anymore."

When I said this her eyes built up and I saw something familiar in them that I, too, felt in my own heart. These weren't tears of sorrow; they were tears of gratitude and contentment. Although she hoped to see her husband again—the same way I hoped to see my Sadie—she knew, somehow, that we had each other until then. Together, even if it was only 30 minutes a day, we made each other feel unbreakable. We felt armored from the world—and all of its troubles—simply by being there for one another.

But even if our "armor" were made of the strongest metal, all metal has its melting point. And Mila's was her daughter, as is any mother's. To see disappointment on her daughters face was a point of no return, heartbreak like no other. And I saw this first hand.

Christmas was coming up and Mila's daughter, Natalie, wanted a popular toy. Mila was excited to get it for her and had, in fact, been saving up. But in November traffic in the diner slowed down—and so did her tips. Without much tips, Mila was forced to decide whether or not she'd pay her bills or buy Natalie's present. She was forced to do the former, and it tore her up. She felt like a bad mother. She felt like a failure.

I, of course, would try to leave her big tips, something like a $20 bill for a cup of coffee here and there, but she never accepted them.

"*Nicholi,*" she would say with a stern voice.

And out of respect for our friendship, I didn't push it. She didn't want any help. I got that.

* * * *

Three days before Christmas, I walked into the diner with a gift in my hand.

Mila placed both of her hands on her hips. "I can't accept this, Nicholi. We agreed that we wouldn't swap gifts. You know this is a hard Christmas for me, as it is."

"You will," I answered, placing the gift on the counter between us.

She looked up at me, rolled her eyes in a cute way and grabbed the gift.

"Wait!" I said, before she began to open it. "You didn't give me your gift, yet."

"Nicholi … I just told you—"

"Do you know what you're going to give me, Mila?" I

kept on pressing.

She didn't understand this sick game I was playing. It wasn't like me to make her feel this low. "I don't have the *money*, Nicholi."

"It will cost you nothing."

She looked at me confused.

"This isn't for you, Mila. Will you please give this to Natalie? I know she really wants it. *That* will be your gift to me."

Mila closed her eyes tightly, put her hand on her chest, and tears streamed down her rosy cheeks. Yet, she shook her head.

"*Mila*, please don't be so prideful. It would mean the world to me if you gave it to her."

She looked deeply into my eyes, but she still said no.

"But why?" I asked.

"Because *you're* going to give it to her," she answered.

Mila guarded her daughter from meeting any men, but now she had given me that privilege. That was the *best* gift I've ever received.

On Christmas Eve, I stood nervously outside of Mila's apartment to meet her daughter. I was more nervous that night than I've ever been walking into the diner. I must have straightened out my clothes and fixed my collar a dozen times before ringing the doorbell.

The door opened.

"Hi," Mila said. "Thanks for coming."

"Thanks for having me."

"What's in the bag?" she asked.

I smirked. "Just a few things."

She gave me a stern look.

I shrugged my shoulders and looked over hers. I saw Natalie playing with her dolls in front of the TV.

"Is that her?" I asked.

Mila nodded.

"Natalie, come here, baby!" she called out for her. And, like most children, she didn't listen the first time. "*Natalie.*"

Hearing her mother's tone, she got up, walked over to us, and she leaned on Mila's leg.

"This is my friend Nicholi. He came to bring you a gift. Isn't that nice of him?"

She stared up at me blankly.

"Hi, Natalie." I kneeled down to her level. "It's *very* nice to meet you."

She hid her face behind her mother's leg.

I pulled out her present from the bag and placed it in front of her, and Natalie peeked from behind her mother.

"What do you say, Natalie? Can he come in?"

She wasn't budging, and I didn't want to force it. "It's okay. I don't have to come in," I said, scooting the gift a little closer to her. "You can still have your present, Natalie.

Santa told me to give to you."

Mentioning Santa got her attention. She stepped away from her mother and stood in front of me. "You know Santa?"

"Yes, I do! Do you want to hear a secret?"

She nodded. I leaned in a little closer to her and then I looked both ways as if I didn't want anyone else to hear, and whispered, "He promised to come visit you tonight."

Her eyes lit up with glee.

Mila wasn't amused by my statement. She didn't want to promise her daughter something that would not happen. But I looked at her and tapped the bag she had asked me about earlier.

Her eyes shrank, and she smirked. *Are you really going to do this?* she asked without having to say the words.

"What time is Santa coming?" Natalie asked.

"Before you go to sleep."

"But how? We don't have a chimney."

She was a very smart little girl, smarter than I was because that detail had slipped my mind.

"Umm, with … his … magic?"

Mila nearly pissed her pants.

"Wow!" Natalie shouted. It was fun to watch her so tightly wrapped in bliss.

"Well, I should go now. I don't want to take up Santa's time with you," I told her. I then got up and mouthed to

Mila to call me before Natalie went to bed.

Mila sent Natalie to her room and closed the door behind her. "You don't have to do all of this, Nicholi. This is too much."

"It's nothing. Look at how *excited* she is."

Mila raised her right brow and crossed her arms in front of her chest. "So what are you going to do until she goes to bed? It's only seven. I usually put her to bed at nine."

Again, I forgot to think about the details. "Well, um, looks like I'm going to have to walk around the block more than a couple times." I laughed at myself, and Mila joined in.

"I can send Natalie to her room," she suggested.

"Please don't do that. I'll be fine." I stepped back and walked hastily down the stairs before she could say anymore.

"*Nicholi!*"

"I'll be fine! See you in a bit!"

Mila shook her head and smiled. "You're crazy!"

I walked for five blocks until I found a park and sat on its bench. Here I was sitting in a park with a bag containing a Santa Clause suit ready to do the whole song and dance to put a smile on a child's face. A few years back, I couldn't fathom such a moment. A few years back, I couldn't fathom *living*.

How did I end up here? I asked myself as I began to reflect on my life. And as I did regularly, even to this day, I spoke to Sadie. "My sweet Sadie, my darling, you are not forgotten," I started out. I say this every day that I wake up and every day that I go to sleep out of guilt that I am living and she is not. But that day in the park, I said it for a different reason. I knew that when I went back to Mila's apartment, it would be a start of a future that would enrich me—and no one had ever filled me with love other than Sadie.

"How can I have a life without you?" I exhaled. "I don't want to move on from you—how could I? You *are* my life. I know no other way to live."

The wind then blew gently across me.

"*Please*, let me hear your voice. It kills me to think that I'm talking to the wind." When I said this, there was a sudden gust of wind and my bag's flap opened, revealing the costume.

I chuckled even though my heart was heavy. "You just want to see me look foolish in a Santa suit, don't you?" I joked, choking up. I held my ear out, hoping to hear even the slightest echo of her laugh in the wind, but no such beauty came. I was heartbroken, but that didn't stop me from continuing to talk to her as if she was beside me. I talked about the good times we had, I asked her to tell Daji I said hello ... and I selfishly asked that she'd stay with me.

I got lost in my thoughts and in my words, and before I

knew it, it was time to head back. It was time for me to start my new life. I got up and asked one more time. "Speak to me, darling. Give me a sign, *anything*. Tell me to stay, and I will."

No wind blew and no voice was heard. There wasn't a single sign of Sadie, but then a memory flashed so vividly through my mind. It was the morning before Sadie told me she wanted to go back home:

She stroked my hair while I slept. I woke up to her eyes fixed on me as if it was the last time she'd ever see me.

"What's wrong?" I asked.

"I had a dream," she said, with a smile that held back sorrow.

"A nightmare?"

She shook her head. "No. It was beautiful."

"What was it about?"

*"It was nighttime. You were sitting on a bench in a park. You cried, you laughed … **you talked to me.**"*

I looked around, anxiously hoping to see her somewhere within the shadows of the night, but there was no sign of my darling. I knew she was there—I *felt* her. And it tore me apart knowing I had to leave her. But I knew I had to do what she asked of me. I knew I had to *live*.

When I arrived back at Mila's place, she quietly opened

the door and I slipped into her room to get changed. While I changed, Mila took Natalie to the bathroom to brush her teeth before bed. Once the coast was clear, I scurried to the living room. I then flicked the living room light on and off twice to draw Natalie's attention.

"Who's that?" Mila asked her.

Natalie ran to the living room. "Santa!"

"Ho ho ho!" I kneeled down and gave her a big hug. "Did my friend Nicholi give you your gift?"

She was so cute. She was too shy to speak but nodded with her fingers in her mouth.

"He's a *good* helper," I said.

"Where's Rudolph?" she asked.

Again, that was *another* detail that I didn't think about. I looked to Mila to help me come up with an excuse, but she was preoccupied with trying not to bust out laughing.

"Umm—" I scratched my head "—he's on ... the roof? Yes! He's on the roof of the building, of course! He couldn't fit in—*but he says hi!* Would you like me to tell him you said hello?"

"Mhmm," she replied, immediately putting her fingers back into her mouth and shifting her body back and forth.

"Well, it was so nice meeting you, Natalie, but it's time for me to go now. I have *a lot* of homes to visit tonight. You stay on that good list, okay?"

"Umm, Santa ..." she said, not knowing how to ask.

"Yes?"

"If I stay on the good list, will you come back with another present?"

"Of course!"

She perked up.

I raised my brow. "Do you already know what you want?"

"Can you bring a daddy?"

I didn't know what to say. She broke my heart and shattered her mother's."

I was speechless and looked up at Mila.

Mila did her best to wipe away the tears from her eyes and called out to Natalie. "Come on, honey." She extended her hand to her. "Santa has to go."

Natalie turned around and grabbed Mila's hand.

I couldn't bear to let her go to bed without an answer. "I'll do my best," I said.

Mila picked Natalie up and signaled me to stay.

After tucking Natalie in, she came back to the living room. She walked up to me, pulled down my fake beard, removed my hat, and stared into my eyes. She adored me. Her eyes said things she couldn't express, but her hand helped her. She gently placed her hand on my chest in a way to direct me to move backward, and I did. She then pointed up to bring to my attention the mistletoe that was directly above us.

"Santa forgot to give me a present," she said, biting her lip and twisting her hips back and forth ever so cutely.

"Is this really how you want our first kiss to be? If Natalie walks out, it'll be like a cliché Christmas song."

She grinned. "Mhmm."

I had stared at her beautiful red lips for months, yet never could I have imagined just how perfect it was to kiss her until I did. It's like life was brought back into me the moment her lips met mine.

From that moment on, we grew to be one very quickly. Time flew by. In the beginning, I'd show up to Mila's apartment for the holidays. The holidays then turned into Friday nights, and Friday nights into Sunday brunches. Within a little less than a year, as planned, Natalie had become accustomed to me being around. In fact, there were times that I had to travel for work and wasn't able to see them for a weekend or two, and Mila would tell me that Natalie had missed me terribly. I felt the same way. They somehow did the impossible—they did something I never would have imagined—they filled the holes in my heart.

Two years into dating, my friend that had become my lover, became my wife. And then ... Levi came.

* * * *

It was a normal night, we (Mila and I) had tucked Natalie into bed and then followed suit. As we lied in bed, I remember seeing this glow—aura, some would say—in Mila.

"Why are you looking at me like that?" she asked as I stared at her.

Her eyes seemed different, yet familiar. I looked away and then back at her. My soul felt like it wanted to leap out and shout for joy, yet I didn't know why.

"What!" she laughed.

"There's something different about your eyes tonight."

"It's called exhaustion," she joked. "Good night, honey." She then, as always, laid her head on my chest to sleep.

I shut my eyes for a minute or two, but my mind wouldn't let it go. I couldn't resist. I *had* to look back into her eyes again to figure it out.

"Honey," I said, tapping her on her shoulder.

"Yes?" she answered, as her head slowly looked up.

My heart sank because Mila was no longer resting on me … Sadie was.

"Are you scared of me?" she asked.

I shook my head.

"You fell asleep. You're dreaming," she answered, knowing what I wanted to ask.

Everything in me wanted to touch her. My hand even hovered over her face as she stared up at me, but I was afraid. I was afraid that if I did, I wouldn't want to wake up. I was afraid that if I touched her, I'd lose my sanity. My love was back and my heart was filled just from the sight of her.

She got up and sat at the edge of the bed with her back turned to me, wearing Mila's silk nightgown.

This can't be a dream, I thought, as I analyzed every bit of her anatomy. Every detail of her was as I had remembered. There was no glitch in this dream. Even the birthmark on the right side of her back just beneath her shoulder was there, as was the beauty mark on her head … and the scars that Mr. Coughlin left.

She looked over to her left, got up and began to walk out of the bedroom.

"Don't leave!" I desperately pleaded, with my hand stretched out for her. She didn't respond and kept walking, so I got up to follow her.

She walked toward Natalie's room and went through her door. When I opened the door, I found her looking at Natalie as she slept peacefully in bed.

"Remember when I was this age and you used to tell me stories?" she asked.

I didn't know what to say.

"I still listen to your stories, you know? The ones you tell her."

My heart was torn to pieces knowing what she was about to say.

"But she doesn't need those stories because she's safe

with you," she continued. "She isn't yours, yet you love her as if she was."

Her words were killing me. There was nothing I could say.

"Levi," she said, looking over at Natalie.

I corrected her. "Her name's Natalie, not Levi, Sadie."

"*Levi*," she said again, with a smile.

I was confused. I didn't understand why she insisted on that name after I told her she was wrong.

Suddenly, everything went black and we were somehow back in my bedroom and standing at the bottom of my bed, looking over at Mila as she slept in sweet peace on *my* chest.

Sadie put her hand in mine and my heart sank again. Her touch was overwhelming real, even the lines in her palm were as I had remembered.

"I know that you love me, Nicky," she said. "But you must love her a little more, for now."

"I … I don't think that's possible," I said.

"You *must*," she insisted, all the while trying to remain composed. "I wish it was different, Nicky, I *really* do. I wish that it was me lying next to you in bed every night, and I wish that Levi was mine."

I turned to her and dared to do what I was too afraid to earlier. I touched her sweet face, and she in turn kissed my palm.

"*Take me with you*," I pleaded. "If this is a dream, then take me in my sleep."

She shook her head. "One day, Nicky. One day I'll come for you, but not today, not for a *long* time. You're going to live to be an old man."

"I don't wish to grow old. I want to be with you now," I cried out.

She rested her face on the side of my neck, and once again, she repeated that name, "*Levi.*"

I then heard a giggle and woke up.

As my eyes opened, I realized that it was Natalie in the living room watching her Saturday-morning cartoons. I got up and made my way to the kitchen where Mila had already started cooking breakfast.

"Someone slept well last night," she said, pointing her eyes up at the clock.

She couldn't have been more wrong. My heart was broken. I felt like I had lost Sadie all over again.

"Looks like you woke up sick, too," she said.

"Too? Are you sick? Is Natalie sick?"

"Natalie is fine, but I woke up so sick this morning. I was dizzy and incredibly nauseas."

"You're not feeling good, again? Why didn't you wake me up?"

"You looked so peaceful," she said, kissing me on the cheek. "Natalie! Come get—" Mila began to call Natalie to get her breakfast, but couldn't finish her sentence. She gagged and ran to the bathroom.

I followed, but she shut the door behind her and locked it quickly.

"Honey, are you okay? *Let me in.*"

"I'm fin—" she tried to speak again. I could hear her vomiting.

"Is Mommy okay?" Natalie sweetly asked.

'She's fine, sweetheart. She's just a little sick right now." I picked Natalie up, brought her back to the living room and distracted her by playing with her and her toys.

A few minutes later, Mila shouted, "Oh my god!"

Fear ran through me, and I ran to the bathroom. "Honey, what's wrong! Open the door!"

The door slowly opened, and Mila looked up at me.

"What's wrong?" I asked, perplexed by her gaze.

She then looked to her left where a pregnancy test rested on the corner of the sink.

"Am I … are you saying … am I going to be a dad?"

She nodded excitedly, smiling ear to ear, and I picked her up and held her like I've never held her before.

Nine months later, Mila gave birth to my only son.

"What's his name?" Natalie asked as she held her baby brother.

We hadn't decided on a name, yet. We wanted to discuss

it after seeing him. But right then and there, I remembered my dream.

"Levi!" I blurted out. "If it's okay with your mother, Nattie, we will name the baby *Levi*."

"I *love* that name!" Mila said. "Do you know what it means?" she asked, excited to tell me.

"No, tell me." My ears were never any more open than in that moment.

"Levi means to join in harmony."

Sadie's message was clear: I knew then that she was still with me.

CHAPTER TEN

∞

"Nicholi, look! I told you it'd come. Isn't it beautiful?"

"It's breathtaking."

"Have you ever seen such a light?"

"Once."

"When?"

"It's like the light that shined above Sadie. The light she chose to step away from for me."

"Nicholi…"

"Yes?"

"Earlier you said that you and your wife had a mutual understanding. You said that you wanted to come back home and Mila let you. I find this hard to understand. How could she let you go?"

"It was time. You see, when you give someone all of your heart and they're taken from you, it never truly empties to make room for another. I adored my wife and loved her deeply, but she was never mine. She always belonged to her first husband, and he to her. And I belong to Sadie."

"Do you remember the day she let you go?"

"It was my birthday."

"Like today?"

"Yes ... like today. I remember that I was sick for quite some time. I remember lying in bed and my wife speaking to me at my side. My children, Natalie and Levi, were at my feet. Mila knew I needed to go home. She told me it was okay. She said she understood that I needed to be with Sadie. And this is the only place I could try to be with her, so I came back here. But maybe she abandoned me the same way I abandoned her."

"Why do you feel that way?"

"I had a life that I always dreamt of having—I had a wife, a home ... children. I was even blessed to be able to play with my grandchildren. I had the life Sadie and I always planned on having, but I shared that life with someone else. I left my darling alone. I lived while she couldn't. How could I do that?"

"Nicholi ..."

"You know ... I've been talking all of this time, and I never got to know anything about *you*."

"What is it that you think you don't know?"

"Where did you say you came from again?"

"I came from the marketplace."

"Then where are your items?"

"I didn't go in."

"Why not?"

"I hoped that my love would meet me there, but he never came."

"I'm sorry to hear that. You're a beautiful girl. I can see that even though my eyes fail me. If he is blinder than me and can't see what you have to offer, then you should move on."

"I'm sure if Sadie was waiting for you, you'd show up, wouldn't you?"

"If I knew where she was and I was able to get there, I'd be there in a heartbeat. *Nothing* could hold me back."

"Is this true?"

"No words I have spoken to you were truer."

"Maybe he's like you. Maybe he sits alone in the middle of nowhere because of his guilt. Maybe he holds himself back. Do you understand what I'm saying?"

"You should go on. *Leave him.*"

"I want you to listen to me clearly, Nicholi."

"*Go on.*"

"They say that in life and *especially* death, people see what they want to see. They also say that when you die your life flashes before your eyes and you relive each moment in a way of your choosing. Sometimes, it ends the way it all started—*with a boy telling a girl a story.*"

"What are you saying?"

"You and I both know that you are not sick and that tea will not help you, nor are you going blind from old age, but from guilt. It's okay that you created a new life, Nicholi. Now forgive yourself so that you can *see.*"

"It's not okay. I deserve to be alone."

"What were the last words you had spoken to Sadie? What did you plead?"

"Why are you doing this to me?"

"Because your guilt blinds you, and your eyes can only see what your soul allows, *so tell me.* As *Sadie* lied beside you in the cold night and life was fading from her eyes, what is it that you asked?"

"I ..."

"*Look at me.*"

"I ..."

"*Tell me.*"

"I said ... wait for me."

"*I did, Nicky. I did.*"

EPILOGUE

"Who's there? Go away!"

"Mrs. Coughlin?"

"Who are you? Who is she? Why are you two in my home! How ... how do you know my name?"

"We're from across the way, just beyond the tall grass. You've been alone for a long time. We'd like to take you to the marketplace."

"Please leave. You torment me."

"Why?"

"You look like a boy I once knew, and she ..."

"She what?"

"She looks like my daughter."

"I look like a boy you once knew?"

"You look like Nicky."

"And who's that?"

"He and my daughter ... they were stitched together from the start."

"What is her name?"

"Her name?"

"Yes. What is her name, Mrs. Coughlin?"

"Her name ... is *Sadie*."

"Would you like to talk about her?"

"I wish to be alone. I *deserve* to be alone."

"I once felt the same way. I was blind just like you, and I was wrong. No one, not even you, deserves to be alone."

"How did you two even get in here?"

"Sometimes doors are shut, but never locked."

Also by J.J. Valentin:

JOHN'S LOVE